M000210142

TEAM SAVAGE 2

Rise of the Pretty Savage in the Crown King

ACE BOOGIE

TEAM SAVAGE 2

Copyright © 2019 Ace Boogie All rights reserved.

No part of this book may be reproduced, distributed or transmitted in any form by any means, graphics, electronics, or mechanical, including photocopy, recording, taping, or by any information storage or retrieval system, without permission in writing from the publisher, except in the case of reprints in the context of reviews, quotes, or references.

Printed in the United States of America.

ISBN: 978-0-9992646-4-5

TABLE OF CONTENTS

CHAPTER ONE

*K*ia sat alone eating at Mickie D's, her mind filled with thoughts of Angel. Her heart was heavy with regret. The only thing holding her together was her plans for the future. She was a millionaire now, with her business bringing in over $700,000 a month. Though she had Money's cheating, lying ass to thank for it all. They had built a network in Madison, Wisconsin, where they sold the finest products the city had seen in decades. It only took a few months to make millions. Everything was going fine until she caught him cheating. She gave him two weeks to confess, and when he didn't, she had him assassinated by Danjunema. The only thing she regretted was Angel being a casualty of war, but sometimes, that was the cost of doing business.

As she ate her food, she picked her phone up and called Danjunema. She was upset with him at the hospital because his man had killed Angel, but she believed he was trying to make her happy.

"Hello?" He answered.

"Daddy I'm sorry," she said, sounding convincing. "I'm wrong for the way I treated you at the hospital," she continued. It was true, she was sorry for acting out on him after all he'd done for her. But the emotions she showed were counter felt.

Her motive for calling was the power he possessed. As long as he craved her, the world was hers.

"Don't worry about it., I understand your pain," he said sincerely. His love for her knew no limits. He understood her suffering. He'd lost his long-time bodyguard, and his two best friends that night as well.

"I'm sorry for what happen to your friends too daddy…. I know it's all my fault."

"Don't put that weight on yourself, what's done is done," he said cutting her off. He didn't want her living with grief on her shoulders. A tear escaped her eyes. His concern touched her heart. She wished she'd given him her loyalty, cause he would've never stepped on her heart. "It's ok Kia, let it out. You don't have to be tough," he said, stressing the words tough.

"Where you at?" she asked. She didn't want to be alone and needed some love and affection to heal her broken heart.

"At home why? You coming over?" he asked, wishing she would.

"Ya, I'll be there in an hour or two," she added, wiping her tears away, before hanging up the phone. When she looked up, a face she'd never forget walked in. She remembered seeing him get into an argument with Danjunema's bodyguards. Kia wasn't attracted to light skin men, but he was fine as hell. He was headed in her direction. She put her head down hoping he wouldn't notice her. They weren't acquaintance, but Kia knew one thing about handsome man: they didn't have a problem talking to sexy woman, and she wasn't in the mood to be bothered.

(Meanwhile)

June took a seat across from Kia and she looked up surprised.

"Do I know you?" she asked with her face frowned up.

"Nah but I know you," he said with a smirk on his face. Kia placed her hand inside her purse gripping her .9MM just in case the past was coming back to hunt her.

"You good ma," June added, noticing her reaction.

"Who the fuck are you?" she questioned while placing the .9 on her lap. June smiled; he liked her style.

"I'm a future business partner who can make you even more money then what's in yo trunk. All I need is a chance to show you. I'm out to be on the top.... If you do business with me, I'll make you the queen of Chicago," he said while handing her a piece of paper with his name and number on it. "Have the African look me up, just in case you think I'm 12," he added before walking away smiling. He fathomed she'd call once she found out he was an associate of Money's brother, Cash.

He got in his car and pulled off with big dreams. The thought of robbing her for the millions in her trunk crossed his mind, but that would be selling himself -short. She was plugged, and in the long run, he'd make more money doing business with her. The moment he got a call from her, his boss Cash would be dead. Killing Cash would make him the king of the land. He had plans on being the next kingpin, and Cash was standing in his way. He thought about his dead brother Killa, and how he was robbed of revenge when Money was murdered. After losing Killa, he lost apart of himself. His mind was in a dark place, a place only revenge could bring him back from, but now the opportunity was gone. He felt guilty moving forward without Money's blood on his hands, but he had to. As long as he kept his brother's memory alive, he'd be happy. He wouldn't be forgotten, like most of the lost souls killed in these streets. His brother was somebody, maybe not to the rest of the world, but he meant something to him.

Damn, why the good die young? It was crazy how he could take a life without remorse, but to lose someone hurt more than anything in this word. When he killed, he never thought about the pain he caused. He wondered if money had any sleepless nights about the murder of his blood. If he was a cold-hearted killer like him, the answer was hell no. June smiled as he got on the highway, heading to see Kim. Just the thought of her brightened his day.

It didn't take long to make it to Kim's house in Beloit. She was his ride or die chick. He had her to thank for his come up. She helped him take over Beloit, and even caught a body to proving her love.

When he entered the house, she was sitting on the sofa, relaxing and watching T.V.

"Hi daddy," she said happy to see him. Every time he was around the world felt so bright. He was everything she dreamed a good man would be and some. "You hungry?" she asked.

"Naw, I'm good ma," he said sitting down next to her. She laid her head in his lap, happy to be under him. "You must've missed me," he joked.

"Naw I ain't miss you, I miss this," she said placing her hand over his dick squeezing lightly. June grabbed one of her breasts and she moaned when he rubbed his finger over her nipple. Kim turned around, and kissed him before sitting on his lap, rubbing her ass against his cock. She felt it harden through his sweatpants. Kim got on her knees and pulled his pants down. His 12-inch dick sprang free. She was about to put him in her mouth, but he stopped her.

"I'm try'na fuck ma," he said licking his lips.

"Ok daddy make me scream with this dick," she said, while turning over on her back and shimmying out her pants. June stood and did the same. He moved between her legs and rubbed the head of his dick back and forth along her clit before putting it in her pussy. She moaned, it felt like heaven. June stroked her slow making sure she felt every inch. He rolled his hips on each downstroke, making her have an orgasm. When it hit, it was nothing short of amazing. Her muscles squeezed as his cock continued thrusting in and out of her. June pulled outta her and flipped her over on her stomach. She felt the head of his cock repenetrate her, and she groaned loudly as his shaft stretched her, in a way no man ever had.

"Damn, ma you got some tight pussy," he said.

"Is it good daddy?" she asked as he pushed more of his dick in her.

"The best," he replied, grabbing a hand full of her ass cheeks, going nice in slow. Her juices kept flowing, and soon she was loose enough for him to give it to her in a faster rhythm. The next thing she knew she was cumming. June kept fucking her through her orgasm, before pulling out and nutting all over her ass cheeks. Kim got up and went to take a shower. June settled back hoping Kia would give him a call. It was only been a few hours since he gave her his number, but he was starting to regret his decision not to rob her. What if she didn't call? He felt like he'd made a mistake, but only time would tell.

(Meanwhile)

Tre Boi sat outside the hospital waiting for Big Ryan. As rain poured down on the car, the storm produced damaging winds. Mother nature was crazy because it started with hot and humid conditions, with only a small chance of rain. But there was nothing hot and humid about this Strom. *It was just one of them days,* Tre Boi thought, as he pondered how the bullet hit Big Ryan in the ankle, then traveled up his leg on the hour drive from Chicago to Milwaukee. They didn't risk taking him to the hospital in the city, frightened of being connected to the body at the gas station. When they wheeled his guy out in a wheelchair, he couldn't help but feel relieved, he hadn't lost another brother. A part of him was tired of the bullshit. He hopped out and helped him into the passenger seat.

"You good B?" he questioned, already knowing the answer from the look on his face. Ryan was normally a playful person, but today he looked down on his luck.

"Naw skud I ain't," he said. A tear rolled down his face, but he quickly wiped it away. The pain inside was unbearable. The streets were becoming overwhelming for him. He was done, it was time to follow his dream and push this rap thing. The heavy rain and wind made it tough to get Big Ryan in the car, but they made it. After Tre Boi helped him, he hopped in and pulled off. They road in silence for a while before Tre Boi handed Ryan a cup of codeine to take the pain away. Ryan took a sip.

"Bro, I'm done my nigga. I can't lose my life in these streets," Big Ryan said. Tre Boi stared, wondering if he was serious.

When he was satisfied, he asked, "What you gone do? All we know is the streets." Big Ryan understood he was right, but he wasn't satisfied with living like this. He felt his destiny was up to him. He didn't wanna wake up in the joint doing life without ever trying to follow his dreams.

"Bro, I'm about to take this music serious," Big Ryan said, and Tre Boi smiled, proud of him. He always believed Ryan would make it if he got serious about music.

"Then do it bro, you know I'm with you no matter what," Tre Boi said. Ryan smiled and stuck out his hand to shake up.

"That's real nigga shit," he said. A part of him thought Tre Boi would've been upset, cause he was losing his partner in crime. But it was the opposite and he was proud to call him a friend. He presumed a real friend would want what's best for you. He was happy to know he found one in the hood. "What the fuck you expect, my nigga? I love you like a brother... Why wouldn't I want what's best for you. I know these street ain't gone show us no love, so we ain't gotta show it no loyalty. Whenever you ready to get out, leave without regret. You don't owe the streets shit," Tre Boi said. Big Ryan let the knowledge his friend dropped on him sit on his brain while they drove back to Chicago.

It was time to change, he didn't wanna end up like so many of their friends. He didn't want his mother to lose her son.

Tre Boi glanced over at Big Ryan deep in thought, and wondered what was on his mind, but didn't ask. He wanted to let him gather his thoughts and make up his mind for the future. A lot of niggas said they was done with the streets, but couldn't quite let go, or worse, the street wouldn't let them go. He thought about how the game was a jealous bitch at times. The few times he saw someone leave the game, they got locked up or killed just before.

They listened to music for the rest of the ride. When they pulled up to Big Ryan's mother's house, she rushed to the car without worrying about the rain. The only thing on her mind was getting her boy inside so she could shower him with motherly love.

After helping Big Ryan out of the car, his mother gave Tre Boi a disgusted stare before slamming the door. Big Ryan looked back and shook his head, before throwing up the Tre's.

"See that's yo fucking problem now." Tre Boi heard his mother say as she smacked his hand down.

He pulled off with a heavy heart. The way Momma Lo looked at him showed she was upset with him.

He understood why she blamed him, even though Big Ryan was a grown man, because his mother did the same. She always thought of him as her lil boy, and his friends were only bringing the worst outta him. Their mothers would never understand they choose this lifestyle, no one was forcing their hands.

He planned to stay away from Momma Lo until she calmed down, he wasn't try'na get cussed the fuck out.

Tre Boi pulled up to his mother's house. Seeing Ms. Lo made him feel guilty for not checking in on his mom the last few weeks. He stepped out feeling naked without his pistol. He gave it to TDN before taking Big Ryan to the hospital. The rain came down and he let it wash over his head as he slowly walked towards the house.

He knocked lightly on the door, knowing his mother hated for people to beat on her door.

"Who is it?" He heard her say on the other side.

"Me, ma!"

"Boy you better say yo name when knocking on my shit," she said, opening the door, with her head cocked to the side.

Tre Boi looked at his mother and wanted to laugh, she still thought she was young. But he decided against it, instead saying, "sorry."

"Boy get yo ass in this house before you get sick.... What the fuck is wrong with you? I swear to god sometimes I wonder if yo sister dropped you on the head, when you was a baby," she said while stepping aside to let him in.

"I love you too ma!" he said, about to enter, but she stopped him. "Take them wet ass shoes off before you come in."

He bent down to untie his shoes, and she slapped him in the back of the head.

Tre Boi laughed. She was really giving him a hard time for not visiting.

"I'm sorry momma, I know I should've been stopping by to see you," he said hoping she'd let it go.

"Whatever boi you act like you ain't got a momma. How come Lo gotta tell me you was with Big Ryan when he got shot?"

Damn, he thought, Ms. Lo must've really been upset to call his mother on him. "That's why I'm here," he lied. "I was coming to tell you, but I guess Ms. Lo beat me to it," he said, leaving his Jordan's on the porch and coming inside. "Ya, whatever you've never been a good liar," she said, giving him a hug. "Boy go change them clothes, you got an outfit you left over. I washed it for you, it's in my room," she said waving him off. He went to get them not wanting to argue with her. He found the clothes before going to take a shower. The whole time during the shower he thought about the chastising he was gone receive, but knew he needed it.

He got out and got dressed before entering the living room where he found his mom sitting on the couch watching TV.

"Get yo ass over here and have a seat," she said without looking at him. He followed her orders without thinking twice. Once he was next to her, she began to speak.

"Look baby I know you grown now and can make yo own decisions. So, don't think I'm try'na tell you how to live yo life. But baby I'm worried about you. Every time I don't hear from you, the first thing I think is something happened to you..." she said while turning to look at him for the first time with tears in her eyes. "I love you baby, and it hurts me to see them streets got a hold on you. I don't want you in em, but I know you yo daddy son, so you ain't gone listen if I told you to give them up. So, I just want you to be safe... If you even think one of them boi's want trouble, you know what to do.... It's better they momma crying then yours," she added.

"I'm not out here playing ma. You ain't gotta worry about crying," he said while hugging her.

She held on tight, praying god would watch over her baby.

(Meanwhile)

"What if I suppressed it and made a vow to never mess with another is it cool for me, to cover my tracks if you'd never know or would me not being honest hurt you more."

Kia sat behind the steering wheel of Money's Bentley reminiscing and crying without shame as she listened to Lyfe Jennings song, "Hypothetically." The heart break and pain inside was unbearable. Every time she blinked her eyes, they displayed pictures of Angel's body in a morgue that haunted her. Tears ran down her face as she thought about her best friend and lover. The night she put a hit on Money was the worst night of her life. She didn't think it out, and wished she'd planned it better. What was she thinking waiting until the last moment to get her outta the house?

When she realized her mistake, it was too late, and she wished she could rewind the hands of time to get her back. She could care less about Money's cheating ass. As far as she was concerned, he got what he deserved. The guilt she felt being responsible for Angel dying too soon was far worse. Her body felt weak without her. Being all alone scared her; not knowing what the future held frightened her.

When she left her house this morning, she thought about going to Madison to see Ne-Ne and Tay-Tay, but she wasn't in the mood to answer any questions. So, she went in the opposite direction and headed for Chicago.

"Hypothetically of course are there some things better left unsaid, or would you wanna know instead, hypothetically of course, are there some wars not worth fighting, some tears not worth crying."

The words of the song spoke her true feelings. Some part of her wished she never saw Money cheating. Life was going great and she was so happy. Her mind told her there were some wars not worth fighting. She pulled up to the Trump International Hotel and killed the engine before she stepped out.

On the way to Chicago she changed her mind about visiting Dajunema. Kia wanted to spend the night alone. She sat in her car with her forehead against the steering wheel. A tear ran down her face as she thought about life and how she had no one to trust. The only person she felt safe with raped her when she couldn't pay a drug debt. Now, she was running to him for safety...something most people wouldn't understand. But Danjunema introduce her to the game. He showed her how to get money, and by raping her, he taught her to always pay her debts, no matter what came up. A lesson she was thankful for.

Kia wiped the tear away and stared at herself in the rearview mirror. What she saw was heartache and pain. Unable to stomach the sight of herself, she opened the car door before slowly stepping out. After pulling the duffle bags from the backseat, she made her way inside.

"Hi, welcome to Trump Hotel, how may I help you today?" the man behind the desk asked.

"I would like a suite," she said.

"Ok, I can help you with that. Would you like our penthouse suite? It comes with…"

"Yes, that's fine," she said, cutting him off in a rush to relax.

"OK you're in a rush, I can tell...Do you need someone to help with your bags?" he asked.

"Yes, that would be nice," she responded.

"OK, I have you set up in our best suite. One of our bellboys will be right over," he said while typing on the computer before adding, "Will you be paying in cash or credit?"

"Credit card," Kia said.

After paying a bell boy to help carry her bags to the room, she stepped inside, threw the bags on the bed, and went to take a shower. Kia slowly undressed before rubbing her fingers through her hair. Her mind was going nonstop. She prayed for it to stop. If only for the night. It would give her enough time to make a plan. She opened the door to the walk-in shower and turned it on. The soothing spray made her forget her worries. It was washing her sorrow away. The hot water felt wonderful, and she relaxed for over an hour. When she got out, she was rejuvenated. The guilt was still there, but she suppressed her feelings like she'd always done. From this moment forward, she would pretend they never existed. With the millions of dollars, she stole, she'd buy a new life. Kia laughed at how she was losing her mind. One moment she couldn't picture life without them, the next, everything was fine.

She thought she was spending too much time grieving, but her body felt differently. Her heart was weighed down and didn't feel like going on, but she wouldn't keep crying over spilled milk.

Her iPhone vibrated and rang at the same time on the nightstand. The screen flashed Tay-Tay's number. Kia pressed the ignore button before ordering wine from room service. She began to get dress while noticing how nice her room was.

She smiled and thought about how just a year ago she was stripping and selling weed on the side. Living in a small apartment and only having a few dollars in her bank account.

Now she was staying in a 10-thousand-dollar a night hotel room, dressing in the best designer clothing, and riding in a Bentley.

Kia heard a light knock on the door. She pulled an oversized T-shirt over her head and went to answer it.

The guy's mouth fell open when he saw how beautiful she was. His glance wandered down to her long legs as he held the bucket of ice with her wine in it.

Kia looked him over. He was a handsome, young African American man about 24 years old.

"Thank you," she said, giving him a tip before closing the door. She popped the bottle and poured a glass, then sat down and took a sip.

She turned on Maxwell's song, "Woman Work" on her phone, and drank a few more cups before getting up and walking around the room restlessly and tipsy. She picked up the phone to order room service again. She got herself a steak and another bottle of wine. She was try'na drink the pain away, before walking out under the stars, and looking down on the cars below from 15 flights up.

Chicago was a beautiful city if you had the money to live outside the ghetto. It was easy to get lost in its beauty when you only saw the high-rise buildings downtown.

She leaned over and wondered how it would feel to jump, to fall to her death. Would she be dead of a heart attack before hitting the pavement? She decided to step back into the room before her emotional state caused her to do something she couldn't take back.

Life wasn't that bad, no matter what happened. Taking her life would be the coward way out. No, she would fight to the end. She would hold strong until she came out on top, or somebody murdered her.

When she walked back in the room, there was another knock on the door. She found the same server on the other end. He had the same lustful look in his eyes as before. Kia's hormones along with being restlessness made her pull him inside. *Maybe some dick could put her to sleep,* she thought, before closing the door.

"I can't sleep...can you help me with that?" she asked, stepping in close to him, so close, he only had to lean forward to kiss her. She returned his kiss passionately, hoping he had what it took to put her to bed.

(3 Hours Later)

Kia jumped up from a nightmare. Sweat covered her body and her heart was beating a hundred miles per hour. Visions of Angel laying in a pool of blood as Kia stood over her holding the murder weapon frightened her. Even though she didn't pull the trigger, she was responsible. Tears mixed with sweat fell from her eyes. She thought the meaningless sex was to help her sleep peacefully all night, but she was wrong. She picked up her phone and called Danjunema, no longer wanting to be alone. He answered on the second ring.

"Hello," he said, half a sleep.

"I need to see you," she cried into the phone. She tried being strong all day, but it wasn't working. At this point in her life, she couldn't be alone. Despite what she tried telling herself, she needed help getting through this. Danjunema was the last person she wanted to see, but he understood the situation. At least he wouldn't ask any questions.

"Ok, where are you?" he asked, happy to hear from her. When she didn't show, he was worried something happened. He had tried calling, but only got her voicemail. For hours, he sat around and wondered how the hit had gone wrong. He wished he could've saved her friend, and his as well.

A part of him wondered what went down inside that house. How did everyone end up dead?

His men were highly trained killers. How had they lost their lives in Milwaukee, Wisconsin after serving in the war in Africa? He heard Kia sobbing on the phone before answering.

"At Trump Hotel," she said.

"Kia, I'm very sorry for what happened to your friend. I never meant for this to happen. I'm sorry for hurting you and I hope you can forgive me. I'm also worried about your well-being. It would be nice if you came to stay with me for a while... how does that sound?" Kia thought about everything.

"Kia are you there?"

"Yes, that sounds great," she said, trying to sound delighted.

"I'm sending someone to get you now," he said before hanging up, not giving her another chance to back out.

Kia laid back and wiped the tears from her face. Maybe it was best to stay with him. No matter how hard she tried, she couldn't suppress these feelings.

(Meanwhile Cash)

The stars shined brightly, and the streets were empty. Beautiful homes lined both sides of the block. Inside them slept some of Chicago's most successful residents. Most of them would lose their mind if they found out a kingpin lived across the street. But Cash could care less what they thought, because 20 minutes ago, he received a call from his mom informing him that his twin brother along with his wife were murdered two nights ago. The news took his breath away, leaving him stuck sitting in his 206 Ferrari 488 GTB in his driveway. He felt guilty for beefing with Money. Now that he was gone, it all felt pointless. All the money in the world couldn't heal his broken heart. Nothing mattered to him now but revenge. He wasn't there for his brother in life, but he would make sure he rested in peace. Whoever was responsible would be held accountable. He pulled his Desert Eagle out and laid it on his lap before pulling off to visit his mom.

It had been years since she allowed him to visit cause of his lifestyle. She didn't approve of selling drugs, or any kind of illegal activities. It shamed her to hear the news of her boys becoming drug pushers.

When they came home that night, she put them out, and they'd been in the streets ever since.

Cash thought about how much he missed her as he drove on the highway. It was a shame his brother's passing brought them together after all these years. Even when his father passed, she wouldn't forgive them for shaming the family name in Wisconsin. He always saw her as a hypocrite for looking down on them for selling drugs, as if she never used herself. When they left Chicago, she got clean and found god. Cash was glad she got it together but was upset she became too holy to have a relationship with them. Even though he was mad at her, he couldn't let the past stop him from loving her now that she wanted to see him. He couldn't make the same mistakes he made with his brother. Cash thought about Money for the rest of the drive, and two hours later he pulled up to a duplex on Raymond Rd. The place made him feel lousy for living in a mansion while his mom rented a duplex. But she refused to live in anything paid for with drug money. Cash stepped out wearing a Gucci track suit and Gucci Bengal slides. The door opened before he was able to knock. His mom stood there with puffy eyes. She looked like she hadn't slept in days.

"Come in baby," she said softly. Cash hated seeing her hurt. *When he found the culprit, they would pay for her pain,* he thought as he walked inside. He looked around the house he grew up in. Everything looked the same. His mom closed the door and tears poured outta her eyes. Cash hugged her, and she cried shamelessly in his arms. Whoever was responsible for her pain would pay. He put that on everything he loved. "It's ok ma, it's ok!" he whispered.

"They took my baby," she uttered. For the first time as an adult, a tear ran down Cash's face. He couldn't stand her pain. They made their way to the living room and took a seat on the sofa. Through her tears his mom smiled at him. She would always be able to see her other son through his face, which made her thank god for giving her twins.

They stared at each other, enjoying seeing one another for the first time in a year. She gave him another hug and held him close. He was her only remaining son. She planned to overlook his occupation and just love him as her son. Losing one child so soon had her questioning her fate. She wondered why god wouldn't take the evil thoughts outta her mind. She wanted blood and prayed for him to heal her broken heart. But them prayers went unanswered, which brought her to this moment.

"Baby I want you to promise me something," she said.

"Anything, just tell me."

"I want them to pay. I want everyone in their family murdered," she said with a cold expression on her face. He never saw his god-fearing mother this upset.

"I will ma, I promise on my brother's soul," he said with tears in his eyes and guilt all over his face. He felt responsible for not having his brother's back. When he thought about it, his brother was murdered while he was too busy pushing him away. He never thought in a million years that something like this could happen to one of them.

How could somebody knock them off when they always stayed on point?

This moment in life was surreal. It was life changing. The kind of moment that gives a person a different outlook on life.

He rubbed his mother's cheek before saying, "It's OK. I'm gone fix this...."

(An Hour Later)

June was laid out in bed thinking of a master plan. He witnessed Kia emptying Money's house, of what he assumed to be millions of dollars. He should've robbed her. But there was a bigger picture to be explored. Why take the money, when she could be his connect? They'd make millions. He knew the Africans were major players from how they moved. If he made this happen, he would no longer need Cash. He could get rid of him, before taking over Chiraq and putting his team on top. All he needed to do was wait for her call.

June peeked at Kim and smiled. She was a real ride-or-die bitch. Everything about her was prefect for him. He was thankful for her changing his life. When they met at a Beloit gas station, he never thought he'd fall in love. She helped him take over a city, and now he was playing with hundreds of thousands of dollars instead of five and ten. June couldn't sleep, so he called Tre Boi, wondering what he was up to.

"What's good skud," Tre Boi said once he answered.

"Shit bro whatchu on?"

"At the spot my nigga, with the rest of the guys. What made you ask?"

"Shit bro, just try'na get into something," June said.

"Shit come through-N-fuck with us."

"I'm on my way, love bro."

"Love," Tre Boi said. June disconnected the line, before getting up putting on his Nike Air Vapor Maxs and heading out the house.

When he stepped outside, the storm was over and the temperature had dropped a few more degrees. He jumped in his 2016 BMW X5 M and pulled off. He flamed up his blunt and turned up the music. As he drove, he thought about becoming the king of the streets. It seemed so close. All he needed was the connect. Then his team could prevail. He saw himself as the new king and thought about the doors he'd open. The freedom and leadership he'd give his soldiers would make him loved instead of despised like Cash. June let his mind slip deep into a daydream as he drove, and 20 minutes later, he pulled up to the spot on Normal. A block before he made it, he pulled his .40 with an extended clip out just in case. It was dark, so he exited the car, walking to the spot with his pistol still in hand. He knocked on the door and TDN answered.

"What's good skud," June said.

"Shit B," TDN said, closing the door behind them. June walked in the back and took a seat next to Tre Boi, who passed him a blunt. After taking two pulls he shook up with him.

"Where Big Ryan at?" he questioned. Tre Boi's face screwed up. "Bro at home he falling back after getting shot," he responded.

"What… when this happen bro?" June asked in shock. He hadn't been around lately, so he wasn't in tune with the block.

"Bro you been missing the action. He got popped at a gas station."

"Damn, a nigga missed a few weeks and all type of shit happen," June added, playing with one of his dread locks.

"This Chiraq my nigga, you know what time it is." June laughed at his comment.

They thought this shit was normal when it wasn't. There was more to life then Chicago, more to life then these streets. He just needed to show them. If he got this new plug, he was going to move them out of the city A.S.A.P. They sat around for hours smoking and shooting dice until 10am the next day. When he left, everybody was asleep.

CHAPTER TWO

Kia

*K*ia woke up in the guest room of Danjunema's extraordinary and contemporary residence. She thought Money's house was nice, but it looked like shit compared to this. The stunning estate was perched on a hilltop. When she entered the handcrafted copper- clad doors, her eyes were drawn to the beautifully designed floor plan. There was a theater and wine cellar, but what she loved the most was the soaring ceilings and the view. Last night, Danjunema was a complete gentleman. She thought he'd want sex, but he did the exact opposite. He told her to take the guest room and wished her farewell. She got up to take a shower. Kia turned the water on as she entered the shower. She thought about the guy from yesterday, and the opportunity of doing business with him. There were so many questions she needed answers to. Like how he knew about her and Danjunema. He seems to have done his homework and that troubled her. She also wondered how he knew where to find her.

He wanted her to have Danjunema look him up and boy did she plan to. If she found anything out of the ordinary, she'd have him murdered. If things checked out, they'd have another conversation. Kia stepped out the shower and changed into a black and red Dolce and Gabbana dress that hugged her body.

There was a light knock on the door and a moment later Danjunema walked in.

"Good morning," he said.

"Good morning," she answered. He walked over and sat on the bed. Kia picked up her Chanel perfume and spread it lightly on her left arm. The room filled with a wonderful fragrance.

"How did you sleep last night?" Danjunema asked concerned.

"Wonderfully," she smiled and said. Last night she didn't have any nightmares or visions of Angel laying in a pool of blood. She got the rest her body needed.

"That's wonderful to hear, I'm delighted to have you in my home. Breakfast will be served in 10 minutes. If you would like to join me that would be nice," he said, standing and walking out the door.

"I would love to." Kia smiled and Danjunema closed the door behind him. Kia felt safe inside his home; she didn't plan on leaving any time soon. She finally made her mind up on what to do with her feelings. She was done crying and needed to get back to making money. Her phone rung on the bed and she picked it up.

"Hey girl," Kia said once she answered.

"Bitch, why you haven't picked up yo phone?" Tay-Tay asked while yelling in her ear. "You had us worried sick," she continued. Kia didn't think about her actions, or how they might impact her friends. When she decided not to answer, she just didn't wanna be bothered.

"Girl I'm ok," Kia responded.

"So, what happened? Who they think killed them?" Tay questioned.

"Girl I'm not try'na get into all that," Kia said choking up a little bit. She held tears back, wanting to put this all behind her. Tay heard the pain in her voice and changed the subject.

"Well, we need you to come through, shit slow down here," she said referring to the block. They needed more heroin. This news made Kia smile. It was time to get to the money.

"Ok girl give me a little while, I'mma call you back when I'm ready," she said. She put the phone in her bag and went downstairs and joined Danjunema for breakfast. When she walked in his dining room, the dramatic glass walls showcased views of the city. Around the corner, she saw a custom-built tasting room with plenty of space to entertain. Danjunema smiled at the sight of her, as the Butler pulled out her seat.

"Your house is really nice," she said sitting down. Danjunema smiled, thankful she accepted his hospitality.

"It's nothing, I have homes all over the world…Why don't you join me? I'm a king looking for his queen, and you're that queen, Kia. Why don't you join me on the throne? And have royal power." Kia responded with a smile, as the wheels of deception turned in her head. He was willing to have her join him and be his queen. She would have all the power in the world with him by her side.

"How can I be your queen if I don't have a crown or ring?" she asked, holding up her hand.

"I'll give you a ring, along with the world, if you'll be my wife."

"So, are you asking me to marry you? Or are you just running your mouth? Kia asked.

Danjunema smiled at her smart remark. He loved that about her. "I'm asking you to marry me," he said.

"Then where is my ring and crown?" she asked.

"I'll have someone take you to get whatever your heart desires."

"Ok, then I'm all yours," she said. Once they were married, she'd begin her reign as queen of the streets. She planned to rule with an iron fist. But first she needed to get her affairs in order. And the first thing on her list was getting June checked out. She stared into Danjunema's eyes as he smiled from ear to ear.

She'd just made him the happiest man in the world. It put a smile on her face to see how much he wanted her by his side. It felt good to be wanted after spending almost a year being a 3rd party in someone else's love story. *Hopefully, with time, she'd make her own love story,* she thought.

"Are you sure about this?" Danjunema questioned. "I understand it's wrong for me to ask something like this while you're dealing with a loss. But the heart wants what it wants.... I've wanted you for some time now, and there's no need in prolonging this conversation. You're my dream woman Kia, so I wanna do this the right way.... If you're not sure, let me know and I'll wait until you are," he continued.

Kia wasn't sure she could love him, but she was sure she'd fall in love with his power.

"I'm OK. This is the reason I wanted Money dead. I wanted to be with you," she lied.

He stood up, then walked around the table to give her a big hug and kiss which she returned with passion.

"I just need one thing daddy," she said, once they broke their kiss.

"Anything!"

"I want you to find out ever thing you can about this man I met. He wants to become a business partner of mine," she said, handing him a piece of paper.

CHAPTER THREE

Three Months Later

S exy wasn't the only word to describe her. Some thought she was fine, others thought she was beautiful. Although all the above was true, they only described her appearance. But words that best described her personality, were not as nice. People said she was cold, heartless, and a savage. But on the outside, Bee was flawless. At five-foot-seven-inches and a hundred and thirty-seven pounds, with a peanut butter complexion and dark eyes, she wowed any person in her sector. Bee's hair was silky, long, and went all the way down her back. She walked with swag and confidence. Her measurements were 34-24-34, giving her just the right amount of ass to drive a man insane. At the young age of 18, Bee was gifted in the looks department, but her life was cursed from the very beginning. Her mother left her outside the hospital when she was only 3 weeks old, and she didn't know her father. She spent all her life bouncing from foster home to foster home, where she learned to steal and fight. The system had its way of growing kids up fast. When she was 14 years old, she learned that her looks would only get her so far, but if she applied her mind with them, she could have any and everything her heart desired.

She also learned at a young age how to manipulate boys, and in no time, she was playing games with their minds. When she turned 16, she met the only family she knew, Black and Glory.

Black was 5'8, high yellow, one hundred and forty pounds with a 40-inch ass. She had blonde dread locks. Glory, on the other hand, was only 5'2, but she was high yellow as well with long hair that reached down the middle of her back. Bee met Black at a foster home and they instantly clicked and became friends. Not much longer after meeting each other, they met Glory and developed a sisterhood that nothing could come between.

What she appreciated about them was how smart and calculated they were at a young age. Bee was older than them by a year. She was the leader of the group. Early in her life, Bee decided she wanted money more than anything else, even love. She showed Black and Glory how to manipulate boys for money, jewelry, and clothes. She made sure their hearts were cold, cause hers was made of ice. She was cold blooded and wanted the girls to be cruel as well. The only thing they needed in life was each other. Trust no one wasn't just a saying, it was a lifestyle. Bee looked across her room, all her things were packed. This was the day she'd been waiting on all her life, but it wasn't how she imagined it. She'd pictured it being the happiest day of her life, but it wasn't. The emotions she felt were far from joyful. *How could she be so sad about turning 18?* She was old enough to leave this hell hole she grew up in. The depression was from leaving her girls behind. She woke up at 2:00am to pack her things to avoid them before leaving. It was only gone make things tough. She grabbed her bags and went to meet Tez outside. He was the key to her future. She planned to use him until she got on her feet.

Tez thought she was the shy good-girl type that you wifed, but he didn't know he was sleeping with the enemy. He was a hustler, a true trap star. With a plug on weed to die for. When it came to pot, he had the streets of Wisconsin on lock and only sold pounds. They began dating a year ago, and for the most part he was a gentleman. He was also the flexing type and told her all his business. Everything she knew about drugs; she'd learned from him running his mouth. And to say she learned a lot was an understatement.

Bee grabbed the last of her things and quietly left the house. She hated leaving like this, but she needed to avoid the emptiness she felt walking out on her friends. All she needed was a few weeks and she'd be back for them. She closed the back door behind her and ran to the car with her bags in hand. She got in and threw them in the backseat.

"Hi, baby girl," Tez said, a big smile on his face.

"Hi daddy," Bee responded, kissing him on the lips. Goosebumps ran all over her the moment their lips touched. Tez was black and ugly, but what turned her off was his weight. He was over 300 pounds.

"Did you miss daddy?"

"I always do," she lied.

"Well we ain't gotta worry about that no more, now you moving in," he said before pulling off.

"Thank you so much for letting me stay with you daddy," she added, playing her roll.

"You ain't gotta thank me, you my future wife, where else you gone stay?" he said rather casually.

"Well I'm gone be thanking you tonight," she said seductively and licked her lips.

"Why don't you thank me now," he said, pulling out his dick. *Damn!* Bee hated giving him head. Even when he was fresh out the shower, he had a scent. *Ok you can do this,* she thought. *I'm doing this for my girls.* She looked over at his dick. It was standing tall, before she even wrapped her hand around his extra beefy 9inch penis. His thickness was always a problem, so she used two hands to jag him off while she sucked on the head and licked his balls. Two minutes later, he nutted in her warm mouth. When they pulled up to the house, Tez grabbed her bags before heading inside. His house was a nice 4 bedroom. Bee spent a lot of time over here within the last year, so she wasted no time making herself at home. "Imma take a shower," she yelled, heading to the bathroom. She undressed and stopped to look herself over. Sometimes she was amazed god had blessed her with a body like this. Then she wondered why he blessed her at all...shit...He seemed to hate her. And he did a wonderful job at making her life a living hell. She turned around and looked at her ass, she thanked him anyways. Maybe her body was the gift that would keep on giving.

She stepped out the shower an hour later and Tez was in bed sleeping. She thanked god; she wasn't in the mood for sex. Scared of waking him, she took her things and got dressed in the front room. She rolled up a blunt, laid back, and started smoking as she watched T.V. Her plans went through her mind. She began to wonder whether she'd have the heart to do it when the time came. The way she felt there wasn't a choice, she had to go through with it, and when the time arrived, she'd be ready. She knew it, it was for her friends. She didn't feel right leaving them alone at that group home.

Their foster dad knew better then to try it while Bee was there, because the last time he almost lost his life. But with her out the picture, it wouldn't be long before he tried to rape Black. Bee hated what she had to do, but it was the only way to save her girls. They had a lot riding on her, and she didn't plan on letting them down. She fell asleep on the couch with a lot on her mind, and with a heavy heart.

*****

"Get up birthday girl," Tez yelled in her ear, waking her from a good night's rest. When she looked at the clock, it was noon.

"Go back to sleep Tez," Bee said while rolling over and closing her eyes.

"Nah fuck all that, get your sexy ass up," he said, pulling the pillow from under her head. "I got a lot planned for my baby's B-day," he continued.

"Ok Tez," she hissed before getting up.

"Ya that's right, get that ass up, get that ass up," he yelled, clapping his hands with a big smile on his face. The way he was acting, she would've thought it was his birthday if she didn't know better. She loved that about him, he really wanted to see her happy. She went to the bathroom and took care of business. She washed her face and brushed her teeth. When she finished, she found a black Prada dress with matching shoes laying on the bed. She smiled because he loved to surprise her. After getting dressed, she walked to the living room and found Tez on the couch, Trued down from head to toe.

"Ok I'm up nigga, so what's yo big plans?" Bee asked, with her hands on her hips. Tez looked her over, she looked amazing.

"Damn you a bad bitch," he commented.

"Who you calling a bitch?" she asked with narrow eyes. She hated when a man called her that with a passion.

"My bad ma, I know how you feel about that word. But I didn't mean it like that. What I meant was you look beautiful."

"Why you just didn't say that?" she joked, and they laughed. Bee thought about how much she liked Tez as a friend. She wasn't in love with him, not even a lil bit. But she did consider him a friend. They always had a good time together even though she didn't like the sexual things they did.

"So, where are we going?" she questioned.

"It's a surprise," Tez said, pulling out a blind fold. Bee's eyebrows raised. "What the fuck is that for?" she questioned.

"I don't want you seeing the surprise before its time," he said. As they drove, she began to second guess letting him blind fold her. It wasn't just him; she just had a hard time trusting anyone. After being abandoned as a child by her mother, she never truly trusted anyone. At the age of 12, she began to wonder why her father never came looking for his child. She also wondered whether he was even alive. It was tough to trust, when at a young age, she learned people could walk out on you at any moment. Even though she believed she trusted her friends, deep down inside she questioned that as well. When he took the blindfold off, they were at the airport. "I know you said you ain't left Wisconsin, so I wanna take you to Colorado for your B-day," he said nonchalantly. Bee placed her hands over her mouth and a tear rolled down her face. She was at a loss for words.

"Come on ma this ain't shit, so stop crying."

"Don't tell me to stop crying, you don't know how much this mean to me," she said innocently.

"Well get used to it ma, I'mma take you all over the world," Tez said with bass in his voice. Bee took time to get herself together before letting valet help her outta the car. When she stepped foot on the private jet, she knew Tez wasn't fronting about how much money he was getting.

Bee took a seat and tried her best to keep her cool. She'd already played herself by crying in front of him. Tez sat next to her an placed a stack of money on his lap." You stay with me ma, this gone become everyday living for you, no lie," he said while handing her a stack of cash, before laying back in his seat and closing his eyes. Bee relaxed as well. She put her seat belt on before they took off. She was scared for her life. When she glanced over Tez was so relaxed, she wondered how often he flew. She felt her ears pop as the jet took off. Bee closed her eyes until it began to feel like they were floating. When she opened them and looked out the window, she was amazed at how beautiful the earth looked from above.

It was the most amazing thing she'd ever seen. The blue sky and clouds under her made her wonder if heaven was this stunning. Bee leaned back in her seat to relax for the flight. She pulled out her smart phone and checked Facebook. It was the same ole shit as always; people posting pictures of themselves living a life far better than their real one. But it was entertaining, so she read their dreams and lies for the rest of the flight. A few hours later they landed in Colorado and checked into the Four Seasons Hotel. Tez left the room the moment she unpacked. Bee thought about how Tez made it seem like all this was for her, but she wasn't dumb. She knew they were here on business.

He talked so much he forgot she knew all his business. The tears in the car were a part of her performance. She planned to enjoy the ride, and her first trip outta state. She spent the day shopping and praying everything was ok with her friends. The money he gave her helped take away her problems for the moment, but not long enough. She made sure to buy them some things as well. They wouldn't forgive her if she didn't. Once she spent all the cash, she headed back to the room to get dressed for her dinner party tonight. Bee laid back on the king-sized mattress and stared at the ceiling. Here she was out of state for the first time, but she was too worried to really enjoy herself. All the shopping in the world couldn't take her mind off the things to come. Things she set in motion. She closed her eyes and took a nap before getting up and taking a shower. After showering she got dressed. She put on a blue Louis Vuitton dress with her hair up.

Bee was beautiful, no questions asked. Tez called to inform her that her ride was outside. A limousine was waiting out front when she walked out the double doors. The driver opened the door and she stepped inside.

She glanced around and loved how nice it was. Tez was rolling out the red carpet for her birthday. She smiled. A lot of today's experiences were a first. Tez was so nice, and anyone could see his love for her. Even though he wasn't the realist nigga or the best looking, any woman would love to be with him, because of his big heart. *It was almost as big as his fat ass,* Bee thought. After thinking it, she regretted it. He'd been a good friend to her. When they arrived at the restaurant, Tez was standing out front. Being the gentleman, he opened her door and held out his hand to help her out.

"You look amazing," Tez said.

"You don't look bad yourself daddy," she said. Bee had to admit, he looked nice in his Calvin Klein collection suit.

"Thank you," he added while opening the door for her to enter the restaurant. Bee was speechless at the sight of them being the only people there. She wondered how much it cost to close the 5-Star Pepper Tree restaurant. As they approached the table, he grabbed a handful of her ass letting it be known that she belongs to him. "Ha, everybody, I want y'all to meet my girl Bee," Tez said happily. Everyone waved, and Bee waved back before taking her seat. As the waiter took their orders, a tall white man walked in. Everyone stopped what they were doing and stood to their feet. Bee looked around unsure of what to do, but stood after Tez stood, giving the man her undivided attention. *"This got to be the connect,"* she thought. He was handsome and put her in the mindset of Harry Styles, with his skinny black jeans and Hawaiian shirt untucked with the sleeves rolled up and his long hair pulled back. Bee wasn't into white boys, but she'd be lying if she said he wasn't fine. "Sorry I'm late. I was tending to some very important business," he said waving his hands for everyone to take a seat, which they did, except Tez and Bee. "Mr. Ryan, I'm glad you joined us," Tez said, shaking his hand before continuing." "I want you to meet my future wife, Bee." Bee waved and took her seat.

"She's even more beautiful in person," Ryan said while blowing her a kiss. When he took the seat next to her, she felt him brush her leg and rest there before giving it a pat and removing it. She gave him a shy smile wanting it to be known she was interested. He stared into her eyes lustfully, wishing she was his. A woman this beautiful belonged with the boss, not a worker.

Bee prayed he was the connect, cause if he wasn't, she was risking losing her sponsor for nothing. But her intuition told her this was the man. She planned to go along with anything that took place. He seemed interested and she was always open to an opportunity to advance in life. When he rubbed her leg with his foot, she knew something interesting was gone take place. Something she welcomed. Bee wouldn't be ashamed if she had to sleep her way to the top. As far as she was concerned, it was a part of the process. It was life as she knew it. The rest of the night, Bee sat quietly and watched them enjoy their time together. They laughed like old friends who hadn't seen each other in decades.

Under the table, Ryan put his hands on her leg a few times, and another time, he placed her hand on his hard dick. The size surprised her. It had to be a foot long and almost as thick as Tez's. Her mouth fell open as he ran her hands up in down it. He stared into her eyes with lust, showing no respect for Tez, lusting over her in his presence. But Tez was too drunk to notice, so she went along with the game.

She pulled her phone out her bag in handed it to him under the table. He got the message, placing his number inside before handing it back. Bee was really turned on by him. For a white boy, he had swag. Tez never saw the exchange because he was too busy running his mouth. He'd become irritating and loud like he always does when he drinks. For him to be such a big man, he couldn't handle his liquor. He was embarrassing. She thanked god it was the end of the night. On the drive back to the hotel, Tez talked the whole ride. They made it to their room by the grace of god. Bee tried helping him, but he insisted he could make it on his own. Once inside, he flopped down on the bed.

"Do you know I'm about to buy 200 pounds from that white mutha fucka?" he asked while laying back.

"I don't care Tez, you told me that 5 times already," Bee said, taking his shoes off.

"I did?" he asked closing his eyes.

"Ya, you did baby," Bee said rather casually. When he didn't respond, she wondered if he heard her. She looked over at him sleeping like a baby. She smiled, and her iPhone rang with a text from Black, wondering why she wasn't picking up. She didn't respond and got in bed with him. On the ride over, Tez conformed Ryan was the connect. She thanked god cause she wasn't sure if anyone noticed them flirting. It would've been a risk that wasn't worth taking. But things seemed to work out. One day she would give him a call, she thought before closing her eyes to get some sleep. Things were coming together better than she thought.

*****

The next morning, they flew back to Madison, WI. It felt good to be home. She loved her first trip outta town but felt homesick being so far away from her friends. Even though they hadn't talked in days, it wasn't the same cause they wasn't in the same town. When they made it to the house, she sat back and got comfortable in her new home. Over the next two days they laid around. Tez was waiting for his weed to arrive then he would hit the streets, but until then he was Try'na keep it cool and lay low. Bee didn't mind laying around one bit because he took good care of her, anything she wanted she got without a problem. On the 3rd day back in town, Tez got up at 6:00am and started making calls before heading out the door. When Bee heard him leave, she knew his weed was here. He always got an early start to his day when trapping. Bee slept until 2:00 PM before getting up. After she took care of her hygiene, she called Black.

"Bitch I'm gone kill you," Black yelled into the phone. Bee smiled "I missed you too girl," she responded, but silence was on the other end. She heard Black crying.

"Did he touch you?" Bee questioned.

"No.... I was just worried about you. You left without saying goodbye. We thought something happened to you girl." Bee felt like shit for leaving the way she did.

"I'm so sorry girl," Bee said tearing up. It was like their emotions were connected. If one cried, they all cried. Bee knew Glory was next to Black crying as well. "I'm going to make it up to you soon, I promise," Bee added, before wiping her tears away. She sat on the phone talking to them for the next 3 hours. They laughed and told stories, enjoying each other's company.

When she finally hung up, she had the strength to go through with the job. Bee began preparing for tonight. When Tez came in at 12:00 A.M holding a duffle bag, the house was dark with candles glowing everywhere, providing just enough light to see her at the end of the hall. Tez smiled with thoughts of the night ahead. Coming home to Bee was a dream come true. Ever since they met, he knew she was the one for him. He was willing to go to hell and back to show his love.

"Are you just gone stand there and look...or come and get this pussy?" Bee asked while taking off her robe and flaunting her naked body. Tez closed the door, taking in her gorgeous curves.

"Here I come, let me put this up first," he responded. Bee turned and walked to the room. His dick twitched at the sight of her fleshy ass. "*Damn,*" he thought as he set the duffle bag in the kitchen. He made his way to the room pulling away at his clothes. As soon as he entered, he sucked in his breath at the sight of Bee naked body on the bed. Bee opened her legs and Tez wasted no time dropping to his knees to marvel at the wet, succulent pussy before him. He began by hugging Bee's hips and planting soft kisses up and down the length of her pussy. It felt like a butterfly was traveling up and down her aroused flesh. Bee screamed and lifted herself up, her breasts swaying as she watched Tez's tongue invade her hot pussy. He began to finger-fuck her slowly, then faster and faster once his tongue found her clit. His fingers were slick and shiny, as well as covered with her juices. Bee was moving her head from side to side. Tez was licking and sucking on her bottom, applying pressure with his lips while his finger plunged in and out her hole. She was groaning and moaning in a continuous expression of pleasure as he brought her to the most intense orgasm, she had ever faked for him. Over the next two hours, they made counterfeit love, until Tez fell into a deep slumber.

Bee got outta bed, her pussy sore from the beating Tez put on it. She made her way to the door naked, letting Lucky and Blue in the front door. Blue kissed her, and they both looked over her body with lust. Blue gave Lucky a look, saying stop staring at my girl, and Lucky looked away.

"He in the back daddy," Bee said licking her lips.

"I got this ma, don't worry. Get dressed and wait in the car," he said, flicking his wrist dismissively. Bee rolled her eyes at him as she rushed to put some clothes on. She felt their eyes on her the whole time.

"Come on Bee you taking to fucking long," Blue whispered.

"Ok, ok, I gotta get something outta the kitchen. Y'all go ahead and handle y'all business," Bee answered heatedly. Unwilling to mess up his chance of getting some pussy tonight, Blue waved for Lucky to follow him to the back. As they walked down the hall, Bee went to the kitchen and took the duffle bag. She tried rushing outta the house, before hearing what happen. "What the fuck!" she heard Tez yell as she closed the door behind her. Tears fell down her face as she went to the car. *Boc! boc! boc!* Bee jumped from the sound of gun shots. She pulled herself together and put on her leather glove before opening the car door and getting in the back seat.

She pulled the 9MM from the duffle bag and placed it on her lap. Her nerves were getting the best of her and she thought about changing the plan but needed to go through with it. Lucky and Blue walked out the house casually and got in the car. Bee put her game face on. Blue pulled off, it was quiet in the car for a moment, everyone in their own thoughts.

"I told you I put in work," Blue said breaking the silence.

"Is he dead?" Bee asked, wiping the tears from her eyes. She'd miss Tez's friendship. It really hurt her heart to set him up, but she had no choice.

"Ya, I put 3 in his head," Blue said with a smile, before hitting Lucky with the back of his hand to get his attention. Lucky reached out and they shook up GD. Lucky went back to staring out the window without a care in the world. He wasn't much of a talker. Blue pulled to a dark side street to dump the stolen car. The moment the car stopped, a shot was fired. *Bloc!*

The impact from the round to the back of the head knocked Lucky's head against the window, blowing his brains all over the dashboard.

"Don't move," Bee yelled, placing the gun to Blue's head. He turned and looked over at his friend's dead body. They'd been friends for all their lives. He was furious and wanted to reach for his burner but knew better. Her hand was shaking, she couldn't help looking at the dead body.

"Damn Bee, you ain't have to shoot folks in the head like that," Blue said with tears running down his face. He wished like hell he could murder her for his homie.

"Fuck you and him pussy," Bee said, meaning every word. He turned abruptly. *Boc!*

Bee shot him in the side of the head. She lifted up and put 5 more in his body. B*oc! Boc! Boc! Boc! Boc!*

Her pussy was drenched from the murders. It felt like she might have an orgasm. She pulled it together and looked around continuously, then tucked her weapon in the bag. The rush she felt inside was something new and she loved it. Bee exited the car and hopped in her 2002 Malibu. It was their getaway car. Bee made her way to Tez's house and took a deep breath before the next stage of the plan. When she pulled past the house, she didn't see any flashing lights, which was a blessing.

After parking the car, a block over, she pulled out her change of clothes that she placed in the back seat a week ago. She changed in case they checked her for gunshot residue. Once she was all done, she placed the other clothes in the trunk, along with the gun and the duffle bag, then walked back to Tez's house where she called the police. The only thing she had to do was convince them they were robbed.

*****

After 5 hours of questioning, Bee was released by the detectives. She felt they believed her story. She wanted to get some sleep so bad, but there was still business to take care of. She took a cab from the police station to U-Haul to get a truck before heading over to the storage where Tez kept his weed. She started laughing once she walked into the storage unit, cause she thought she needed a U-Haul, but there was only about a dozen big duffle bags, she thought 200 pounds would be a lot bigger. Bee unzipped one of the bags and saw it was packed with loud. She took her time with loading the bags in the truck. She so casually went about doing it, that a person would never guess she was doing something illegal.

After she was done, Bee headed over to her duplex on Raymond Rd. Once she unloaded the smoke, she put it in the basement. She was dead tired from all the work, and staying up all night, so she decided it was best to get some rest before she made a mistake. Thoughts of Tez came to mind and she got sad. When she started her plan a year ago, she never thought he'd become a friend. From the day they met, she planned on robbing him.

Blue was a boy she met at school with something to prove, so she played with his heart and got him to kill to prove his love. When the police found their bodies, they'd have no choice but believe that the 3rd robber Bee made up had killed them to keep the money for himself. Over the last year she used the money Tez gave her to get her own apartment under the table. She fell asleep with her girls in mind. When describing Bee, it was best not to get lost in her appearance, cause the word that best describes her was savage!

CHAPTER FOUR

*T*hree months past and Cash wasn't any closer to finding his brother's killer. It felt like searching for a ghost. He hadn't heard any gossip, and no one was revealing any rumors or reports of an intimate nature.

Thoughts of his promise to his mother came to mind, and keeping it was all that mattered now.

He stared at his team, as everyone awaited his orders. They were meeting to declare war on Big G, to avenge Money's murder and the killing of his soldier from the first war.

He was done giving passes. If you violated anyone on his team you had to go, he thought.

"Today is a new day...a day of change. It's the day I put brotherhood before all else. Today I want to apologize for my short comings as a leader...I apologize for making it tough on y'all to get this money. From now on, anybody with the motivation to hustle can. It doesn't matter if you a hitter or hustler no more, everyone can eat. From now on it's about us! I'm gone stand and go to war with y'all, and that's why we're here...I got a hundred pack on Big G's head. I want it done on sight. The person that gets em, gets access to as much coke as they can handle," Cash said before glancing around the room.

"I'm declaring war on all opps! You see an opp, you hit em. Is that understood?" He asked. They shook their heads letting it be known they understood. "Good, y'all can go," he said before exiting the room with bodyguards.

He planned on turning a new leaf, becoming a better person for his team. It was time to show love to his hitters and to everyone in his crew. Gone were the big I's and little U's. Everyone would get the opportunity to become a boss in their own right. He was getting old and it was time to find his successor. He needed to crown the next king and let him take the throne.

But there were some problems. Could he live without the fame? Without the spotlight? All questions he didn't have the answers to.

(Kia)

Kia set on a private jet headed to Africa. She was going on vacation to hand pick mercenaries to protect her once she returned to the states. Her life was going great. She married Danjunema two months ago and things were wonderful. As a wedding present he gave her 50 keys of raw heroin along with a black card. The world was hers, and she was acting like it. She also had Danjunema research June and learned he was a friend of Cash, Money's twin brother. Kia never liked him. She disliked how he treated Money, and how he played Money after he was released from prison. He wasn't loyal, and since June was a friend of his, she planned to stay far away from him. They didn't have any type of business future. Now that her life was upgraded, she made sure to do the same for her partners. Ne-ne and Tay-Tay sold weight now, and One Eye Larry ran the Trap house.

It was crazy how the right plug could turn a hype into a middleman. The game was fucked up like that.

Kia felt like her heart was in a better place. She wasn't having nightmares anymore, even though her love for Angel was still strong. She missed her every day, but the pain lessened over time.

She wondered if they'd meet in heaven. That thought made her laugh, cause she already knew that the devil had a place waiting for her in hell.

She didn't care about her soul, but prayed Angel saw the holy gates. She wasn't just an angel by name, but by heart.

Kia looked at her husband and smiled. She'd grown to love and admire him as a leader. The love he gave her without desiring anything in return showed her what true love was. Their sex life wasn't great, but it was a small matter as long as she had her 10-inch dildo, she named "Money"

His sex game was the only thing she missed. But sex didn't make the world go around, dollars did, which was something her husband had so much of, that they'd never spend it all in this lifetime. They were visiting his county, and he planned to show her that not all Africans lived in huts, some lived like kings. But the trip wasn't only about sightseeing, they were on business as well. He come to invest in real estate. Danjunema loved bringing opportunities back home. He wanted Kia to see the bigger picture when it came to the game.

She needed to learn it was about getting ahead, and not about spending every dollar on material things. He used a lot of his money to invest in the African community, to uplift his people.

Even though he lived a lavish lifestyle, he gave back almost as much as he spent. He wanted his wife to experience poverty in the belly of the beast, and show her that where there was a will, there was a way.

Kia was happy with her lifestyle. She was at ease with her past and wanted to leave it behind her. Danjunema planned to spend the next few months in Africa, something she didn't have a problem with. After all the problems she had, she just wanted to kick her feet up and relax, at least for now.

When she made it home, she'd get her money for the 50 keys before unleashing her mercenaries on the streets of Wisconsin.

*****

June left the meeting with confusing emotions about Cash, who seemed like a new man. It was hard to believe he could change. Once a snake. always a snake. Some things never change.

Cash was still the old cash, he thought.

Months passed without hearing anything from Kia. He regretted deciding not to rob her when he had the chance. But a part of him held out hope that one day she'd give him a call. But for now, it was time to get back to the money. When he walked outside, Kim sat in the car waiting. He got in the passenger seat, reclined it, and laid his head back.

"You OK daddy?" Kim asked as she pulled off. She saw he had something on his mind. He peeked over at her, fortunate to have her in his life.

"Ya I'm good ma...Cash seemed different today, that's all."

"Different like how?" she asked, keeping her eyes on the road.

"I can't put my finger on it, but something changed."

"Don't over think it, just go with yo instincts, they'll show you the way."

June loved her with all his heart. She was his soulmate. He didn't have to tell her what he wanted, she seemed to always know. With her by his side, the sky was the limit. There was nothing like having a strong woman at yo side. His mom used to tell him this, but now he believed it. He was experiencing it firsthand. Kim gave him her all, followed his lead, and never questioned his judgement. He was contemplating on popping the question but wanted his mom's approval. He planned to get her opinion the next time he stopped by her home. But for now, they'd keep thuggin it.

(Meanwhile)

Tre Boi pulled up at the spot, his mind on the $100,000 that Cash had on Big G. He planned to collect it tonight.

Big G fucked with one of his hoes. She told Tre Boi everything they did to get close to him. He was gone have her set him up for 20 bands. He picked up his iPhone and called her.

"Hi boo," she answered.

"Fuck all that, I got a move I need busted."

"OK...what kind of move?"

"I need Big G tonight, got 20 on em."

"You can get god for that."

"You know that," he said laughing at her joke.

"Where he meeting me?" she asked, getting straight to the point. The only thing on her mind was dollar signs.

"Have him pull up on yo block tonight."

"Cool. After it's done, I'm getting outta town. You know them niggaz gone go crazy over this, so hold my cash until I get back. I ain't calling for a month. So, don't play with my shit boy!"

"This me, you know I won't play with yo cash. How many times we done this?" he questioned.

"Too many times boy. I was just fucking with you, so get out yo feeling," she lied.

"Ya want to be on the block by ten," he said hanging up the line.

Just like that, he'd be plunged with cash. Once Big G was gone, he'd make it snow.

He stepped out the car, walking in the trap house. One of his workers was weighting up ounces of coke on the kitchen table as a girl held a blunt to his lips.

"What's good skud?" Tre Boi asked

"Them 3's," he responded.

"True," he said, walking to the back and stepping into a room filled with smoke. The rest of the guys sat back playing 2k. "I got next," he said, taking a seat.

"We playing 2 bands a game," TDN said.

"So, what that mean? I still got next...... You know what, I got 5 say you don't win this game." Tre Boi said as TDN hit a 3 pointer with LBJ.

"We on."

The next 20 minutes, he smoked a blunt and watched TDN beat the shit outta Monty. When the game was over, he pulled out 10 bands, counting off 5 and handing it to him.

"Pay me in full. Shit, you know better than going against the king," he said, putting the money in his pocket without counting it. He didn't have to, they never played each other.

"Ya whatever nigga, I don't know shit bout a king if it ain't Dave," Tre Boi replied.

"Ya all that."

"Ay, I'm gone need you tonight. I got Big G in my sights."

The whole room came to a standstill. "No bullshit?" TDN asked.

"No bullshit, but we gone only get 40 bands a piece. Gotta pay the bitch who setting it up," he said while rubbing his waves. When he looked up and saw the hungry facial expression on some of the people in the room, he regretted bringing up such a big hit in front of them without being able to give everyone a taste of the score. He knew they needed the money, but TDN was the best man for the job. Other than June, he was the best shooter.

" Man, we can do that bitch as well. You ain't gotta give that bitch 20 bands for shit," TDN said, unable to wrap his head around paying a t.h.o.t that kind of money.

"Nah skud, she one of mine," Tre Boi said, unable to have her murdered. She was an asset to him in more than one way.

"Damn, fuck it then. Shit, I can use 40 bands."

"You know that scud," Tre Boi said shacking up. "We gone stay here until it's time, then it's show time," he added.

(2 Hours Later)

Kia touched down in Johannesburg, South Africa. It was beautiful, and she'd never imagine this in her wildest dreams.

Whenever she saw Africa on TV, it looked dry and poor, but now she was looking at paradise.

At that moment, she knew this would be her second home. Once she locked down the drug game in the Midwest, she planned to move here for good. She looked around at the attractive woman walking around with almost nothing on. She glanced at Danjunema; his eyes were on her.

She smiled. He never paid attention to another woman. He made her feel like the most stunning woman in the world.

"It's gorgeous here," she said staring out the window.

"It's nice here. The only thing gorgeous is you," he said from his heart.

"Thank you," she spoke softly, loving that every day he went out his way to show her love. He'd stolen her heart and healed it all in one motion. He was becoming her king, and she was already his queen.

The sun shined down on them making it really hot, but the AC kept them warm inside their car.

"I could stay here forever," she said, amazed with his country. "You can! We could do whatever you like. I've already told you that when I asked you to marry me."

Kia smiled at him, before leaning over to kiss him on the lips. "I still got business in the states...And so, do you," she said, reminding him of their empire back home.

Once she made it home, it was the beginning of a new day in Wisconsin. It was time for the State to have its first Queen pin. She felt that anything a man could do she could do better, and she wanted her city to know it. Milwaukee was her pride and joy, but no one knew she existed on the drug trafficking stage. But that was about to change in a few short months.

While her mind was busy daydreaming, they pulled up to a mansion unlike anything she'd ever seen. It was a next generation masterpiece, an exquisite modern marvel of engineering & design. When they crossed the floating footbridge and she saw the grand double story entrance, she fell in love with the place. She stepped out and followed her husband inside. White marble tile and hand scraped hardwood floors greeted her. The place had an infinity-edge swimming pool, a lighted tennis court, a fully equipped gym, a spa, a theater, a resistance pool, a wine cellar, a guest house, an underground ballroom with catering kitchen, formal and informal gardens, and so much more. She loved it. The next few months here would be more lovely she thought.

(That Night)

Tre Boi and TDN sat in a stolen car down the street from Jessica's house, waiting for Big G to pull up. The music played low in the background as they sat quietly in their own thoughts.

TDN held an AK47 in his right hand pointed at the floorboard. "Bro we been out here 3 hours already...I don't think he gone show up," he said rubbing the firearm.

"Nah, he gone show up, this little bitch got the best head in the city," Tre Boi responded. Not even a moment later, Big G's Lexus parked a half a block away. TDN pulled his ski mask down, before rolling down the window. He sat up in the seat.

"Pull up and block him in," he told Tre Boi. He slowly pulled up until they were side by side. TDN raised the AK and pointed it at his head. Big G looked up into the cold eyes of a killer.

Boc!Boc! Boc!Boc!

The window to the Lexus exploded and the sound of the AK could be heard blocks away, as the first round soaked into his upper body. He slumped over to the passenger side. TDN lifted himself out the window firing more rounds.

Boc!Boc! Boc!Boc!

He watched as Big G's head and body was clobbered with bullets. When he was positive he was in hell, he sat back in his seat and Tre Boi slowly pulled off.

"Now, Blue and the rest of the guys can rest in peace," he said turning up the music. Tre Boi smiled, thinking how big of a hit they'd just committed. They'd be admired by Cash for pulling this off so soon.

(Meanwhile)

The lights in the house were low and soft music came from the kitchen. June watched T.V. in Beloit while Kim made him something to eat. The only thing he wore were boxers after 2 hours of passion. 24-hour boxing was on the T.V. His phone started to ring. When he glanced down at it, he saw it was Tre Boi calling.

"What's good?" he answered.

"I need you to link me with Cash. We just got fat bastard."

"No bullshit?" June asked, stunned to hear the news. He knew the nickname they had for Big G. He couldn't contain his joy as a smile spread across his face. Kim walked out the kitchen, wondering what the commotion was about.

"Everything OK daddy," she asked, a baby 9mm in hand. When he saw her clutching, he smiled. He'd turned her into a savage.

"Ya, I'm good ma, my bad for raising my voice."

"This yo house, you can do as you please daddy," she said, playing her role and making sure he felt like a king. He made her dreams come true, so it was nothing to do whatever he wanted. He watched as she walked away with her naked ass on display. Thoughts of following her in fucking came to mind, but he didn't, Tre Boi words stopped him, bring him back to the conversation at hand.

"Ya it's done. Got him a little while ago."

"Good shit skud, I hope you know what this means?" June asked.

"Fucking right I do…It means we can get our hands on as much work as possible," Tre Boi responded.

June loved how he use the word "we" and "our." It showed his loyalty. Even though he made the kill, he was a team player. When they started hustling, June put them on. Tre Boi loved him like a brother, his loyalty was with team savage. It was them against the world.

"You know that," June laughed.

"You know what, why don't you tell Cash you got dude out the way. That should help you get a little closer to him. After this you should be in there like booty hair…But I'm gone need that money though," Tre Boi said.

"Nuh skud, I can't do that," June protested.

"Look skud, I know you got something up yo sleeve that's gone change our lives. I know what it is and I'm try'na help, that's all," he said.

June couldn't believe the selfless act Tre Boi committed on behalf of brotherhood. It showed he was willing to do anything to put this team ahead.

"Damn skud! That's real nigga shit," June said.

"You know that. Just get at me when you got that paper. I can do without the glory."

"You understand nobody can know about this. I can't have Cash second guessing me," June said.

Lying could get them killed if Cash thought they were disloyal. "The only person that know is TDN, and he with me right now. I'mma put him on game when I get off the line with you. Bro with us, so he on whatever we on. His mouth ducted taped, he won't make a sound.

"Good looking on this move bro, you don't know how much this gone help."

"Nah nigga I do. But, get with me when you get a chance. I ain't try'na be on this phone talking to you like you my lady n shit," Tre Boi joked.

June laughed before hugging up on him as Kim walked in with his plate. She gave him a kiss before going upstairs. He sat there watching Floyd Mayweather prepare for his upcoming fight. He loved boxing; it was the only thing he watched on T.V. His thoughts wandered to killing his big homie. It was becoming a tough decision since he seemed to be leaving his snake ways behind. June thought about the good years when Cash was around more often. The days he went to war with them. But all that changed when he became the king of the city.

His brother's passing seemed to remind him life wasn't promised, and anyone could get it. Life was too short to be fighting with loved ones over bullshit. He wanted to end this plan to kill Cash, but a part of him felt it was too late

He'd robed a few of Cash's trap houses and even killed a few of his soldiers. His team was waiting on him to take over and become king. No one said it, but everyone wanted Cash gone. They wanted a king they believed in, one they related to.

He remembered the days Cash was on the battlefield, but most of this soldier didn't. In June they saw a leader who stood toe to toe with his team and went to war with his hitters. To them, Cash was too far removed from the hood, he was a rich nigga, just another old head who couldn't understand the struggle. It was time for the crown to be placed on a new skull. He couldn't let them down, but he was thinking that maybe he wouldn't be able to go through with it if Cash straightened out his act.

He still had love for Cash and only wanted him gone if he tried standing in the way of him providing for his soldiers. But that was no longer a problem. He'd opened up the door for everyone to get money. June knew deep down, he didn't have a reason to kill him.

Fuck it, he thought. If Cash stayed true to his word, he'd abolish his plan of taking him out.

*****

Bee slept the full day away. When she got up, it was 12am. She got off her living room floor and felt pain all over her body. *"Damn,"* she thought as she headed to the bathroom to clean herself up. She looked in the mirror, saw her reflection, and smiled. She even looked attractive waking up. As she stared, she also spotted something new, something dark. What she saw was a cold-blooded killer. The thoughts of the double homicide only turned her on. But Tez's murder was difficult to think about, so she acted like it never happened. He just didn't exist anymore, she convinced herself. It wasn't her fault. After taking care of her hygiene, Bee retrieved a cab to the Malibu. She paid the driver and stepped out to a night that looked lovely. The stars and the moon looked bright. She took in a deep breath accidentally, but it seemed to calm her nerves. Now wasn't the time to be bullshitting. She had to execute this stage of the plan peacefully. She didn't need any trouble. If she got pulled over, it could be the end of her life.

So, she wouldn't make a mistake. She got in the car and drove to the Sheraton Hotel on John Nolen Drive. Bee stepped out and removed the gun from the bag with her leather gloves, before beginning the long expedition to the lake. After the 20-minute walk, she held the weapon in her hand for a moment. The power she felt was unbelievable, and for a second, she thought about keeping the murder weapon. But her better judgment kicked in, and she threw it in the water. She thanked god it was done. As far as she knew, there were no witnesses to the crime, and the murder weapon was now gone. She was free to chase her dreams, without any fear of going to jail.

It was done. Her plan worked and now she could relax. Bee pulled her phone from her pocket and dialed Black. She told them to get ready. The excitement in their voices put a smile on her face. Bee pulled up at B.P. by Allied, a Westside landmark in Madison. If someone in the underworld came through the Westside, they stopped there just to see who would pull up. When Bee stepped out, everyone gave her their full attention, something she was accustomed to. Bee didn't pay them no mind, as she picked up 3 scales before heading to the foster home. When she pulled up, Black and Glory were waiting outside. They climbed in smiling.

"I told ya'll, I was gone get ya'll outta there," she said. Black began to cry, making an ugly crying face. It was the worst.

"Thank you," she said while giving Bee a hug. Glory sat in the back quietly as tears ran down her face, lost for words. She never thought Bee would come this fast.

"You don't have to thank me bitch," Bee responded, wiping the tears from her eyes. She was glad, and this was a moment to celebrate. It was their first time together free...well kind of free.

"I'm so happy to see you bitches," she added before pulling off. They were only kind of free because Black and Glory were considered runaways. They wouldn't be able to attend school or have any kind of police contact until they turned 18. Once they arrived at the duplex, Bee helped them carry their bags inside. The duplex was 3 bedrooms, 2 bathrooms with a full-size kitchen. There was no furniture, just 4 chairs and a table in the basement. It wasn't much, but it was home to the 3 girls who never had a place to call home. When you have never had shit, you appreciate the small things. Glory let Black pick her room first. She knew if she didn't, they would have argued for hours before Black let her choose. After putting their things in their room, they sat on the living room floor.

"So, what's next? Is Tez gone pay the rent, or we on our own?" Black questioned.

Just hearing Tez's name mentioned damaged Bee so much. "We on our own, like we always been...But we have each other, and that's all we need," Bee said. They stared at each other a moment, just happy to be together.

"I told ya'll we sisters. I'mma always take care of ya'll," Bee added. She saw the anxiety on their faces, and for a moment she saw who they really were scared kids.

"What about money?" Glory whispered.

"We ain't got to worry about money for a while," Bee whispered back as a joke. Glory always acted like someone was listening even when they were alone. Bee stood to get the duffle bag. She returned and poured the money on the floor. The shook expression on their faces was priceless.

"Where did you get all this money?" Black yelled, grabbing a few stacks.

"Don't ask questions you don't want the answer too," Bee commented with her hands on her hips.

"Have we ever kept secrets?" Black asked, her face screwed up and her eyebrows raised. Bee knew the look, because she had seen it many times before. If she didn't answer the question, Black wouldn't let it go, so she said fuck it.

"If I tell y'all it stays between us!" They didn't respond, just shook their heads. "Ok here we go," Bee said taking a deep breath. She believed sharing this information could send her to prison, but she trusted them with the secret.

"Tez is dead. So is Lucky and Blue." Bee paused, but Black waved her hands for her to continue.

"Girl give her a second," Glory said with sympathy.

"No, I'm ok...I lied when..." Bee struggled to get the words out. "I lied when I told y'all I was gone use Tez to get me an apartment. The real plan was to rob him."

Glory put her hand over her mouth, halting the questions she wanted to ask.

"Blue and Lucky killed him," she added through tears. "And...and...I killed them," Bee said.

Glory sat on the floor, lost for words. When she heard the confession, she wished she never did. She wanted to ask why but didn't. Black stood up and gave Bee a hug.

"It's ok," she said while wiping the tears from her face. Glory stood and hugged her as well.

"You never have to lie to us. We family, and family look out for each other," Glory said, forcing a smile to show support.

"I didn't want y'all to worry," Bee cried. They sat and hugged each other for a while. It was moments like these that forged their friendship. Moments like these, made them feel loved for the first time.

"Ok now that's enough of all this soft shit," Black stated, fucking up the moment like always.

"Bitch you the reason we can't have nothing nice," Bee said, smacking her lips. Glory rolled her eyes. Black was just crazy like that. Most people didn't like her off first impressions, but once they got to know her, they saw through the tough girl act, and saw a lost soul that was looking to find a way.

"Girl, you know that hug was a little too long, the only thing I'm try'na hold onto that long is a dick," Black said.

"We know that fo show, that's all yo lil fast ass want," Glory laughed.

"And you know this," Black said, throwing up her middle finger.

"Well let's count this money," Bee said, rubbing her finger together.

They went down to the basement and laid the money on the table.

"Girl I can't believe this all ours," Glory whispered. Black and Bee stared at her and rolled their eyes.

"Once again little girl, ain't nobody down here you don't have to whisper," Black joked.

"Ya, ya, whatever bitch," Glory yelled. They all took a seat and began counting the cash. After numerous miscounts and even more jokes, they finally had a total of $200,000 in cash.

"Damn that's a lot of money," Black said, putting her hands over her mouth.

"Oh, my fucking god," Bee shouted. She took a hand full of bills in threw them in the air.

"Girl I can't believe this shit, we all got $65,000 apiece," she added as the money rained down on them.

"Wait this ain't our money. Bee, this yo money," Glory commented. Bee frowned up her face.

"Look bitch if you say some more crazy shit like that, we gone have to get it in. You know me better than that…Everything I've had since we met has been y'all as well. From clothes, to money, ain't shit changed," Bee said angrily. Glory hurt her feelings. She didn't like the idea that her friend thought money could change her, and for a moment it made Bee second guess their friendship. Glory saw the pain on her face and wished she could take her comment back. Bee was a great friend, and never switched up.

"I'm sorry girl, that came out the wrong way."

"I hope so," Bee said firmly, still upset. Her nostrils flared and her eyes narrowed. Black stared at them both. "And y'all say I know how to fuck up a moment, you bitch's crazy, I got 65 bands in my hand for the first time. I don't know about you hoes, but I'm turned on right now," she joked, and everyone laughed. That was Black for you, always willing to lighten up any situation with a joke.

"Ok now we gotta weigh this weed," Bee said casually, as she opened one of the duffle bags. The smell of the weed escaped the bag like runaway slaves.

"Damn, that shit smell good," Black uttered. They began to weigh the weed and put them into pounds, which added up to 140 altogether. Once they were finished, they celebrated by dancing and making it rain on each other. By the time they fell asleep, it was 4am.

(Cash)

Cash was with Dria, lavish, Lesa, and Barbie getting a massage. They catered to his every need, and in return they lived like queens. A small price to pay to be royals. It was an even smaller price to pay when they would've done it for free.

He'd met them through Dria. They had an orgy and over time they all fell in love with him. Since his brother died, they'd been spending more time with him. Every night, he slept with one of them, making passionate love and confessing his feelings. He gave them promise rings, promising to always keep it real with them, and to never lie about who he was fucking, or about his feelings. To some hood bitch, this was romantic.

His phone rang, and Dria handed it to him. June's number flashed across the screen.

"What to it skud?" he answered.

"Them Tre's."

"You know that."

"I got some news fo ya. I got fat bastered," June said nonchalantly. Cash sat up in his seat, waving his hand for them to leave. Once they exited, he said, "You got em?" Unable to believe it.

"Ya!"

"Good shit my nigga," Cash said, happy with his best hitta. He believed someone would get him, but never this soon.

"You know that skud."

"I'mma get up with you first thing in the morning. I'mma have that cash ready too. But we gotta kick it too my nigga," Cash said.

"What about skud?" June asked, confused with his nerves getting the best of him. What if somebody told Cash that Tre Boi made the hit already.

Thoughts of Cash setting him up came to mind. "Damn my nigga, I gotta have a reason to kick it with my nigga?" Cash asked, sounding a little disappointed. Was he that far removed from the team? That nigga felt uneasy around him now? Had he become that self-centered over the years? June used to be like a little brother, so if he felt Cash needed a reason to come kick it, he could only wonder how the rest of the team felt.

"Nah I ain't saying it like that. It's just been awhile since you had time other than business, that's all my nigga," June said.

"Ya I know, but those days are behind us. So, you gone kick it with the big hommie or what?" Cash asked.

"You already know!" June replied.

"Then see you tomorrow. Love broski."

"Love bro," June said before hanging up the line. Cash was delighted to hear the news about Big G. The war ended before it even started. He planned to take on the rest of the gangs as well. He wanted the streets to be theirs alone. If he couldn't find out who killed his twin, he would take it out on someone. So, why not the competition? *But that would be selfish,* he thought. It wasn't right to put his soldiers through war, cause he was grieving. Doing that would be another injustice to them, something he'd done a lot of lately. No! He would lead with compassion. Why make war, when you could make money? *There would be no more senseless killing,* he thought to himself before calling his girls back in the room to party.

(The Next Morning)

Bee was up by noon thinking of a whole new plan. She got up to ponder while Black and Glory were still asleep, and the house was quiet. The original plan didn't involve taking the pounds. She thought he'd have all cash, but her timing was off. Tez ended up reupping on her birthday. He sold out faster than normal. Bee stared at his trap phone in her hand, debating whether to use it to get rid of the weed. It was the only way to turn it into money. She thought long and hard about the best solution to this problem but kept coming back to the same thing. She knew what the weed was worth. Tez showed her the game one night and she never forgot. The problem was getting niggas to respect her. They'd try her playing the game at this level. There was a lot of money in her hands, and with it came problems. Bee learned that she didn't have a problem taking a life to get what she wanted. She thought about her life, and all she'd been through. What did she have to lose? Nothing!

Bee pushed the power button, turning the phone on. *It was time for better days*, she thought. They'd been through enough. It was time to get this money by any means. But her girls had to have her back to accomplish this goal. They need to be colder than any man in the game. Bee was willing to do anything to live a lavish lifestyle, even if it meant killing. Something about the thought of murder turned her on. It was like taking a person's last breath gave her the power of god. Bee couldn't do this alone.

She woke Black and Glory up to get their opinions. "What you want?" Black yelled half asleep, rubbing her eyes, trying to wake up. Black was a deep sleeper and got pissed when she got woken from her sleep. Glory, on the other hand, can get woken up from the smallest sounds. Glory sat up on the floor and stared at Bee like she was crazy.

"What you want Bee?" she spoke softly, wiping her eyes.

"I need to talk to y'all," Bee said as Glory shook Black.

"Get up Black, damn!" she said. Bee laughed at Black, staring at them like she wanted to fight before setting up.

"Bitch what I tell you about touching me when I'm sleeping," she said annoyed.

"Well get up then," Glory said, standing her ground. Bee looked at them both; they were crazy. But she wouldn't trade, them for anything in the world, not even a million dollars.

"What you sitting there smiling about bitch?" Black asked.

"I'm just happy y'all here that's all."

"Bitch that bet not be the reason you woke us up," Black said with a screw face.

"Nah it aint, I wanna run this idea past y'all…it's about our future," Bee said. "I got an idea, but I wanna know if y'all had plans of y'all own," she added.

"I haven't given it much thought," Glory said while looking to Black. "Me either, but I'm with you. Shit you're always the one planning."

Bee looked at her girls and shook her head, she loved how they trusted her to plan their future but wished they didn't depend on her so much. What if something happened to her, and she left them on their own?

Bee pushed the thought out of her mind, not wanting to think it into existence.

"Well my idea is to sell weed…" she announced.

"What?" they both asked, confused. They knew Bee would do anything for money but dealing drugs hadn't been one of them.

"Just listen, we have to take care of ourselves we on our own now…money has to come from somewhere," Bee said while looking at them.

"But we have money, we don't have to sale weed," Glory whispered.

"How long you think that money gone last …. All I'm saying is this, we've lived our whole life going without, stealing clothes, fucking to get a few dollars out a nigga. This is our chance at a new life. This is the fucking jackpot," she said, holding up the phone. "All I need y'all to do is have my back and trust me. When I say can't nothing go wrong, it can't…y'all know I think shit through, that's why y'all trust my plans, cause they always work. I've thought long and hard about this and it's planned out to a tee," she said, pleading her case, while staring intensely at them. She could envision the money as if it was already in her hands, all she needed was them to agree. If they didn't, she wouldn't do it.

"Nothing can go wrong?" Glory questioned. Bee thought about the things that could go astray, the possibilities were endless, but she wouldn't tell them that. "No!"

"I'm positive," she said, lying to them for the first time that she could remember.

"Girl I'm with you," Black said.

"Me too," Glory added.

"What we gotta do now?" Black asked. Bee stood up and looked at the ringing phone in her hand. She couldn't wait to get to the money.

"First, I gotta make a few runs on my own, cause you lil bitch's hot. What I need y'all to do is stay put until I get back. Do y'all want anything while I'm out? she asked.

"Some Mickey D's." Black said, getting up to use the bathroom.

Bee looked at Glory, and noticed she looked worried. Bee knew that if hustling was going to affect anyone, it was going to be Glory. She was the opposite from them in so many ways. Black and Bee skipped school to hang out with boys. Glory got good grades, and never missed a day. Bee hated bringing her into this, but she needed them now more than ever. She made a mental note to get Glory out as soon as possible.

"You need anything sis?" Bee asked Glory.

"Mickey D's is fine," Glory spat out the side of her mouth. Her mind was all over the place at the moment. Overnight, her life had changed. She went from being at the top of her class to a runaway and a drug dealer. She worked so hard to make sure her life didn't turn out like so many young African American kids who grew up in poverty, but overnight that all changed. The look on Glory's face made Bee feel guilty about everything she'd been through because Glory truly had a good heart. They used to predict how she would change the world.

"Don't worry sis, I got y'all, you should know that by now...Have I ever put you in harm's way?" Bee asked softly.

"No," Glory responded through tears. Bee walked over and hugged her, before kissing her forehead.

"What's wrong girl? What's on your mind that's got you crying... if it's selling weed, don't worry about it. Me and Black will do the hard work, all we need form you is this," Bee said while pointing at her head. Glory thought different from them, and her mind would keep them on point and grounded. Her fears would always give them another way of looking at things. It would keep them from rushing into shit that could land them in prison. Glory wasn't street, but sometimes it was good to have a L-7 on the team.

"It's not really that. I don't wanna be a drop out…you know I wanted to attend college more than anything," she cried, making Bee tear up.

"I know, I know," she said while holding onto her sister. "But you can't go back to that house, it's too dangerous," she added. Tears flowed down Glory's cheeks, and Bee wiped them away.

"You gotta be strong. As soon as you turn 18, you can go back to school. This is not the end of your story, it's only the beginning. When you're famous, they'll love hearing the story of a strong woman who overcame poverty and became a success." Glory laughed at Bee. She was good with words.

"I'm ok, I'll be fine," she said while smiling and wiping the tears, try'na be strong for her best friend.

"You sure?" Bee asked with sympathy.

"Ya."

Black walked out the bathroom. And screwed her face up at the sight of them hugging.

"I know y'all bitches ain't have a moment without me?" she joked, and they laugh.

"Let me go take care of this business," Bee said, standing to leave.

Bee spent the next few hours shopping for furniture and getting everything, they needed. She picked up 3 iPhones for them. She picked up dyes for Black and Glory's hair, a black one for Black's dreads and a honey blonde for Glory. They needed disguises to move around and fake IDs as well. Once Bee was satisfied, she had everything, she headed home. When she returned, Black was seated on the floor as Glory oiled her locks.

"Bitch you took all fucking day. You got us in here starving and shit," Black said try'na sound convincing as she took the food. Bee glared at Glory, she was in a better mood and it put a smile on her face.

"Here sis," Bee said, handing her the new iPhone. Glory's face lit up. She loved technology, and if anything could lift her spirit it was this.

"Thanks sis," she said, giving her a hug.

"Where mine at?" Black asked, with a sad expression on her face, and her bottom lip sticking out.

"It's in the bag bitch…I don't know why you worried about a phone, ain't you starving?" Bee asked, smacking her lips.

"I am," Black said, taking a big bite outta her Big Mac. She walked over to get her phone out the bag, and one of the dyes fell out.

"Who this for?" Black asked. *Damn,* Bee thought.

Bee was hoping to bring this subject up later because Black was sensitive about her hair.

"Oh, ok hear me out" Bee began, but Black was putting two & two together, and shook her head. "No!"

"Y'all need to dye y'all hair."

"Bitch you got me fucked up. You must've lost yo muthafucking mind!" Black yelled, cutting her off. If there was anything, she didn't play about it, it was them damn locks.

"Look girl you a damn runaway now. The police are looking for that ass, and it won't be hard finding a hoe with blonde dreads," Bee stated, her hands on her hips.

"She right," Glory added while taking a bite out her Big Mac.

"I hate y'all hoes," Black said, throwing the dye across the room and running upstairs.

"Love you too," Glory yelled.

"Girl stop playing with fire," Bee said, knowing Black needed time to herself, and Glory teasing her would make things worse.

"Ya you probably right, I aint try'na fight that girl over her hair," Glory said, understanding where Bee was coming from.

"While that girl has her moment, I'mma need you to use that mind of yours to find some fake ID's on the black market," Bee spoke while looking the other way. Glory was a beautiful nerd, and she knew her way around a computer. She'd dated a hacker just for him to teach her everything he knew.

"Ok I got you," she said, using her iPhone. It took only a few minutes to find what she was looking for. Bee walked around the living room. She couldn't wait for the furniture to arrive. The house was too empty for it to be comfortable.

"I found it! But we gone need to dye our hair first for the pictures," Glory said.

They fought with Black for another hour before they dyed their hair and took the pictures. Once she was done, Black liked her new look, even though she still hated them. Glory's new style looked magnificent; the honey blonde looked great on her. After arguing and changing their hair styles, they laid around on their cell phones, but Tez's trap phone kept ringing. It was tough for Bee not to answer the phone, but she wanted to wait for the ID's to come. She needed to take Black along without worrying about her getting locked up. So, for now, the money would have to wait for just a little longer.

"Ok I was just thinking about selling weed, and if we gone do it, we gotta be smart about it," Glory said outta nowhere.

"Look at my girl ready to go all in," Black laughed, but Bee didn't! She gave Glory her full attention.

"No, for real, selling weed is big business in Colorado. I was reading an article about how it's a billion-dollar business. We should approach it like a business. We can open up a clothing store and sell pounds out the back." Bee looked at Glory smiling from ear to ear.

"Ok girl you right, but let's take it a step farther. Let's open a bar or a night club with a weed dispensary in the back," Bee said, standing to her feet. She was charged and ready to get started.

"I aint the smartest bitch in the world, but won't the IRS want to know where we got money to start a club?" Black asked. All the energy running through Bee's body escaped at once as she thought about the new-found problem at hand. *Why didn't she think of this?* she wondered. Bee took a seat before laying back on the floor, her vision of being a night club owner was smashed under the weight of her body. Glory waited a moment before revealing something else she learned on the dark web.

"I might know how to make a paper trail, to make it all look legit," she said. Bee sat up again.

"Ok what do you mean you might know how? I need to know if you can before I get my hopes up again," Bee said, crossing her fingers and closing her eyes, and praying to hear "yes."

"I can," Glory said. When Bee opened her eyes and looked at her friend, she wanted to kiss her, but instead gave her a hug.

"Ok so that's the plan. We gone sell the rest of the weed off the phone, and when we are finished, I'll meet Tez's connect and try getting more. Hopefully, a variety of different kinds. If everything goes well, we'll open up the club and stop selling pounds, leaving us with the best smoke in Madison and possibly Wisconsin," Bee said.

"Girl yo ass is something else!" Black said, rolling her eyes while giving her girl a high five. Bee thought about how this could change their lives. They could get rich.

"I'mma need a computer if I'mma work on my part of the plan. This smart phone won't be good enough for all the things I gotta look into," Glory said, breaking Bee's train of thought.

"Ok, just make a list of what you need and I'll get it. Time is money," Bee added, snapping her fingers.

(Chicago)

Inside a Mercedes Benz, laughter was in the air as the two friends joked about the murder of another human being. The day before, June had set up a meeting with Tre Boi to get all the details about big G murder. When he was satisfied, he'd be able to convince Cash he was the shooter, he set up the meeting.

"I got that $100,000 in the back," Cash said, unable to breathe from laughing too hard.

"Ya I need that too," June said, passing the blunt. His dreadlocks got in his face, forcing him to pull them into a ponytail. He glanced over at the big hommie smiling and laughing with him like old times. It felt good to sit with him and relax. Over the years, Cash had become hostile.

June learned that no one was safe around him. He could smile in yo face and have someone shoot you in the back of the head. June knew because he'd seen it before. Seeing this type of behavior made it tough to trust him.

He put hits out on friends and beat old ladies over a few bands. At times he could be heartless, untrustworthy, and brutal. He took them to war without once thinking about their lives being on the line.

But lately something seemed different. His eyes didn't seem as cold. Instead, there was pain in them from the loss he took, but other than that, he was changing.

"Good work bro! I gotta say that. We gone fall back in the city right now. No more war. Niggaz down here respect us, they know how we get down. So, we ain't gotta stay on front street. We can lay low and relax. I want y'all to take time to get y'all money up, while I look into the murder of my peoples..." Cash said, his voice telling off. Thoughts of his brother almost broke him. June felt guilty having the information Cash wanted, and for being unwilling to hand it over. It wasn't time just yet; he needed a little longer.

CHAPTER FIVE

2 Weeks Later

T wo weeks went by fast, as the girls tried accomplishing their goals. The ID's arrived, so Glory and Black were able to get some much-needed air. Everything was moving along until they had problems with the club. It was hard getting a liquor license. They were at the end of a two-year waiting list. One thing Bee learned while in the system about white folks, is that in their world, money moved things along immediately. If the cash was correct, you could get almost anything. Glory found them a lawyer to help them skip the waiting list and speak their language. At this very moment, Bee was headed to his office. She parked her car and hopped out to go inside.

"Hi how may I help you?" The blonde secretary asked, reclined at her desk.

"Yes, I'm here to see Martez Reynolds," Bee said in her most professional voice.

"Do you have an appointment?" The blonde asked without glancing at her.

"Yes, I do," Bee said rolling her eyes, not feeling her vibe.

"Ok, well have a seat. He'll be with you in a few minutes," she said while picking up the phone, still without looking up at Bee. Bee waited 5 minutes before being called back. When she entered his office, her mouth dropped. Standing in front of her, was god's gift to woman. Martez stood 6'4 inches tall, weighed around 225 pounds, and favored NY Giants receiver Odell Beckham Jr. The only difference was his hairstyle. He wore waves. He was the finest person she ever laid eyes on, besides herself of course. Her mouth was still open as he reached out for a handshake. Bee closed it and tried staying professional, keeping her mind on business.

"Nice to meet you Ms. Gamez," he said in a deep voice, as they shook hands.

"It's nice to meet you as well Mr. Reynolds." Martz took a seat behind his desk, and Bee followed.

"So how may I help you Ms.Gamez?" he asked, resting his elbows on top of his desk while staring into her eyes. She looked away, afraid to get lost in them, and forget the reason she was there.

"Ok, so I'm not sure where to begin, because this is all kind of new to me."

"You began by telling me why you're here," he said, cutting her off.

"Well I'm looking to open up a night club, and I'm having trouble getting my liquor license. I wanted to know if there was a way around the waiting list?" she asked, all in one breath.

"Wait, let me make sure I understand what you're asking. You want to know if there's a way to skip the list, right?"

"Yes," she answered and swallowed hard. Her nerves were getting the best of her. She felt nervous around him, and uptight about her role as a businesswoman. These feelings were new for her and she began to second guess herself.

"Let's speak hypothetically for a minute. If there was a way to do what you're asking, it would cost a lot of money," Martez said. Normally he wouldn't entertain a conversation like this, especially with a person he didn't know, but the pain and the struggle in Ms. Gamez's eyes came from the streets. She was beautiful on the outside, but the eyes told a different story. They looked inside a person's soul, and her eyes had hood written all over them. "How much money are we hypothetically speaking about?" Bee asked, letting him know she understood. He rubbed his hands over his face and stared into her eyes once more.

"First a person would have to make a few calls, and verify that you can be trusted, then I'd get back to you," he said, without breaking eye contact "But again, this is hypothetically speaking," he added.

"Ok then," Bee said, standing to leave. Martez stood as well, and they shook hands before she left. The moment she stepped out the door, she thanked god she was able to speak with him. Something about him took her breath away. His hands were so soft, and inside his eyes there was something deeper. When she looked into them, she saw he'd lived that lifestyle at one time or another. She wasn't sure, but she'd bet at one point in his life he either hung with street niggas or was one himself. Bee got inside her car, and pandora read her thoughts. Tamia's "Almost" began to play.

"Can you tell me"

How can one miss what she's never had?

How could I reminisce when there is no past?

How could I have memories of being happy with you boy,

could someone tell me how this could be, how my mind pull up

incidents, recall date in time that never happened, how could

I celebrate a love that too late, and how could I really mean

the words I'm about to say.

Bee laughed at herself as she pulled off. While in Martez's office, she found herself wondering how it would feel to be in his arms. How it would be if she was his women.

I miss the times that we almost shared, I miss the love that was almost there, I miss the times that we use to kiss. At least in my dreams let me take my time in reminisce. Bee sang along to this song on repeat as she drove home. When she pulled up, she was still jamming. She rushed in the house to talk to Glory about what had happened at the lawyer's office. The furniture and everything arrived last week. The house was no longer empty. Bee knocked on Glory's door before entering. Glory sat in the same place she was when Bee left. The only difference was her clothes.

"I should have never got that computer," Bee said while taking a seat on the bed. Glory turned around and faced her. "I'm try'na make sure things are in order to keep us safe," she whispered. "I know baby, I'm just fucking with you...but I'm mad at you," Bee said, smacking Glory's leg. "For what?" Glory asked, raising her eyebrow.

"Bitch you could've told me that lawyer was so damn fine!" Bee said smiling.

"Bitch that was a business meeting, not a date."

"I know, I know, but I walked in his office and my mouth fell open, and my heart skipped a beat," Bee said happily.

Something about the moment made Bee believe in love at first sight. Glory laughed at her girl until she saw the look on her face.

"Oh, you not playing?" she asked. Her eyes were beyond wide as she waited for a response.

"I really think I might like him. I don't know," Bee said surprised.

"No, no, hell to the no. You can't like him. He might be a business partner of ours. So, listen Bee, I know he fine, but that's not why I picked him. I did a search on the dark web, and he has a fucked-up past," Glory said, giving her girl the tea. Bee held her chest in shock.

"What's fucked up about him? Don't tell me he a rapist," Bee said, holding her breathe waiting for an answer. Glory paused a moment keeping her silence. Bee felt her heart about to jump out her chest, it was beating so fast.

"It's a long story that I'mma tell from the beginning!" Bee shook her head waiting to hear more.

"Ok he's 35 years old..."

"He's 35?" Bee said, cutting her off. Glory smacked her lips.

"Damn bitch let me spill the tea," Glory said. Bee got quite again.

"Ok bitch, so when he was in law school, him and some friends went out clubbing, and there was a fight. It began inside the bar but continued outside. When they got outside, shots were fired, and someone got killed. Some people pointed the finger at Martez, but others said they thought the man was darker. As the police were about to arrest him, his best friend confessed. Bee sat there with her mouth in her chest. "The friend should be on his way home. After the confession, he changed his story but still lost at trial. Martez worked on his case, and he got a lot of time back from the state. But rumor has it that Pretty Boy was the one who committed the murder. They say his friend confessed because he had a future ahead of him," Glory added.

"That some shit outta a movie," Bee said, standing up and rubbing her fingers through her hair.

"But that's only half the reason I picked him. He's from the mud, off the south side of Chicago. His mom was killed by his father when he was 13. He grew up in the system like us, and he's young and hungry, just what we need," Glory boasted.

"Glory you my bitch," Bee said, bending to hug her. "Always thinking some next level shit," she added.

"I know one thing, you hoes been doing a lot of hugging. Let me find out y'all gay," Black said while entering the room.

"You always thinking, and this hoe always talking," Bee said, pointing to Black.

"I be thinking, just not about the same shit as ya'll hoes. The type of shit on my mind is how much them new Jimmy Choose cost, or I wonder if he got a big dick," Black said, and they laughed uncontrollably for a minute or two. Bee wiped the tears from her eyes.

"The bitch is crazy," she said in between deep breath.

"Insane is the word for me bitch, crazy don't cut it," Black said snapping her finger.

"Girl be quiet and get ready. We got shit to do," Bee said chuckling.

"Like what?" Black questioned and cocked her head back.

"I'm about to text everyone outta Tez's phone and let them know we back in business. We gotta get this money cause when I talked to the lawyer, he said we gone need a lot of money to skip the waiting list.

"Well start sending the mutha fucking texts," Black said, throwing her hands in the air and flicking her wrist dismissively.

"Little girl you crazy," Bee laughed, taking Tez's phone outta her pocket before sending a group text. It said: *Back in business, don't call, text orders.* Messages began coming in at once. One was for 10 pounds, another for 15, and two for 50. Bee couldn't believe most of the pot could be gone in a day. What Bee didn't understand was how the two weeks wait had the clientele wanting as much as possible. In case it happened again, they didn't want to run out.

"Oh my god," Bee said, looking at the phone.

"What's wrong?" Glory jumped up worried. This whole hustling thing wasn't for her. Ever since they began, Glory was jumpy, and on edge before anything illegal even happened. They planned for Glory to work on the legal aspect of business.

"It ain't shit bitch. It's good! We should be done with everything in the morning if everything works out," Bee explained. She watched as Glory relinquished the worry, and a smile replaced it.

"Quit playing bitch," Black said excited.

"No lie," Bee confirmed. Black jumped up and down. She thought about everything she wanted and couldn't contain her happiness. "We about to be rich," she yelled. Bee was shocked. She didn't know the exact math, but if they sold all 135 of them at $2,500 a pound, they should make around $300,000 in one day. Her pussy got wet just thinking about the life they'd live making this kind of money. Bee stopped thinking about the future and calmed herself down. They needed to make the money first. Just as she plotted on Tez, someone could plot on her. She needed to be ready for anything. If she wasn't, it could be her taking 3 to the head. Before making any moves, she needed to get another pistol. If a mutha fucka tried something stupid, she ain't have a problem murking them.

After planning everything with her girls, she went to her room. They'd meet the four buyers tomorrow at different hotels to avoid attracting attention. After making the deals, they'd leave within minutes of the buyers, never to return. Bee called an old fuck buddy of hers.

"What's good," he answered on the 2nd ring.

"Nothing really," she said with sex appeal.

"What you on, I know you only call for one thing," he said nonchalantly. Bee smiled and rolled her eyes. He was right, she usually called for good dick. But that wasn't the case tonight.

"Nah, not tonight. I'm calling on business," she said, try'na keep her mind off the D.

"Stop playing girl, you know what business I'm in. What you gone do with one of those?" he asked with hesitation in his voice. Bee smiled an evil smile, just like a nigga to think she wasn't a killa. She'd bet he ain't have two bodies under his belt.

"I got money, that's all you need to know," she said mockingly.

"Where you at then?" He asked, always a businessman first.

"Meet me on Westbrook in 30 minutes," she replied.

"By Raymond?" he asked.

"Ya." Bee hung up the phone and threw on her black jogging suit. She waited 20 minutes before starting the short walk over to Westbrook. When she arrived, he was already waiting inside his car with the lights off. She knocked lightly on the passenger window. He sat up and unlocked the door.

"Hi," she said getting inside.

"Bee you sure you know what kind of business I'm into?" he asked, unable to believe a woman this fine, was try'na get her hands-on illegal pistols.

"Ya boi."

"Ok cool, then this all I got right now," he said, pulling 2 baby nines from under his seat. Bee looked them over and loved how they felt in her hands, not too heavy, not too light. They looked like twins. The only difference was one had an extended clip.

"I want these two, and another one of these," Bee said.

"What you got going on girl?" he asked all in her business.

"Nothing you need to worry about…but I need another one of the clips as well," she added pointing to the 30 clips.

"Here," he said pulling his 9 from his waistband and switching the clips giving her another extendo.

"Ya this right," she said looking at her twin bitches.

"Girl you look good as hell with them extendos. I'mma start calling you pretty savage," he laughed. Bee didn't hear him, as she was in her own thoughts at the moment. "The only extendo you need is this," he said. When she peeked over, he had his dick in his hand. She loved the sight of it but wasn't trying to mix business with pleasure. At least not tonight.

"Boy how much do I have to pay you?" She said letting it be known she wasn't interested. He put his dick away getting the hint.

"Give me 650 for both." Bee pulled out her money, counted off $700, and handed it to him.

"Thank you," she said, placing the guns in her bag before exiting the car. When she made it back home, Glory and Black were asleep. She put the guns under her bed before laying down. She thought about the name Pretty Savage and decided to call her twins 9 MM Pretty Savages. She laughed inside before falling asleep.

(Kia)

The light from the moon lit up the room. Kia felt the wind on her back as it blew through the window. She rode Danjunema's small dick for everything it was worth.

She normally faked orgasm, but tonight he seemed to be hitting all the right spots. She didn't know if it was the dick, or how she'd grown to love him. They say that love makes sex better, and tonight, she was becoming a believer. Tonight, it was amazing. She felt an orgasm building deep within. When she glanced down at her husband, his eyes wear closed, sweat covered his face. He was having the time of his life. She came the moment she saw his face. He was handsome, a true man of power.

"I'm cummming, shit daddy, I love this dick!" she yelled, when she cum. Danjunema was right behind her. She jumped off him and rushed to put him in her mouth. She sucked down every drop of his love juices.

Once his cock went soft, she released it from her lips. Danjunema laid there speechless, and outta breath. Kia laid next to him, and he held her in his arms. She felt safe with him. The last few weeks were great. She'd found her mercenaries, and her army was coming together. When she made it home, she planned to released them on anyone standing between her becoming queen.

The men she found in Africa fought in wars all over the country, so the streets of Milwaukee would be a walk in the park.
She looked over at Danjunema, he was sleeping like always after she put the pussy on him.

Kia stood up and went to the bathroom. She got a towel and wet it with hot water, then went to wipe his dick down. When the hot towel touched his penis, he opened his eyes and looked at her before closing them again. This was a nightly thing. She took care of him like a king, cause in her heart he'd become one. Life was crazy like that at times. She used to hate him, but now he'd proved his loyalty, he'd proved he could be trusted with everything, except one secret.

Danjunema came back into her life at a time when she was hurting, and in need of love. What she didn't know, when she began her plans to use him, was how a person can enter your life at just the right moment and change everything. Her broken heart opened her up to any man willing to heal it.

Kia placed his limp dick down, pulled the cover over him, and went to take a shower. She stepped into the shower and turned the hot water on. The spray of water seemed to calm her nerves. Every night when she showered, she thought about Angel, and sometimes even Money. She missed them. Kia missed how Money made them feel like a family. He showed her things she'd never seen, exposed her to a life she never lived. Her success in the game was due to his leadership. What she missed most was Angel's friendship. The way they took care of each other was special. Their love was deep within their souls, it was one you could easily spot.

"Damn I can never get her back," she thought out loud.

Kia spent over an hour in the shower reflecting on the past before getting out and putting on her robe. When she entered the room, Danjunema's back was to her. He didn't see her enter as he was on his phone.

"Keep an eye on her. If anything happens to her, I'll kill you myself. I spent a lifetime looking for her. If anything happens, it's not only your life on the line but your whole family. Is that understood?" he yelled into the phone, before hanging up.

"Is everything OK," she asked him.

"Ya everything OK, it just business," he said, laying back in bed. "Come, let's sleep," he said waving her over. Kia got in bed feeling a little uneasy. Something was up with that phone call, she just wondered what.

(The Next Morning)

Bee and Black woke up first thing in the morning and got to business. They'd already met with 3 of the buyers without any issues.

Bee also talked to Martez this morning and was meeting him in an hour. When it came to the buyers, the plan was that Black would appear to be in the hotel room alone, while Bee sat in the bathroom holding her pretty savages. If customers took care of their business and left, they never meet Bee. But if they didn't, she'd show them what a pretty bitch could do. A part of her wanted someone to act up, to make an example outta them. She was ready to take the game by storm, and anyone standing in her way. A knock at the door brought Bee back to the business at hand. They needed to make it through this final sale to relax. She went in the bathroom as Black opened the door. A strong tall man walked in. He looked like an NFL player, instead of a drug pusher. He was the biggest man Black ever laid eyes on, and his locks hanged down to his ass.

"Where Tez at?" he asked in a deep voice, sitting down like he owned the place. Black looked at him and prayed to god he wouldn't start any problems.

"He couldn't make it, so he sent me," Black stated. It was the line she'd used all morning. The man shook his head.

"What's wrong with nigga's now a days? How he send a bitch to sale a nigga 50 pounds? Like I won't just take his shit," he said. He quickly grabbed Black around the neck and slammed her head into the wall putting a hole in it. The force almost made her pass out. She couldn't breathe as he choked her. Black grabbed his arm trying to remove them from her neck, but he was too strong. Bee heard noises and stepped out with her 9's ready for action. "Pussy let her go," she yelled, aiming the gun at the back of his head. He looked over his shoulder before slowly raising his hands in the air. "Walk over by the window," she ordered, her heart beating along with her pussy. She wanted to kill him so badly, it turned her on. She kept him at gun point as he walked to the window. Black was stuck to the wall unable to move a muscle, unable to believe all this was happening.

"Come on Black, get the weed," Bee said. But Black didn't move, she stayed on the wall with her hands in the air. "Grab the bags," Bee yelled snapping Black outta her daze. She ran taking the bags off the bed.

"Take them to the car and come back to get the rest," Bee said, waving one gun over her shoulder at the door. Black rushed out the room.

"Bitch nigga lay your bag on the bed and get face down on the floor," Bee said, stressing the words "face down." He placed the bag on the bed, before slowly getting on the ground. He thought about putting up a fight, but the look in her eyes told him otherwise. The money wasn't worth his life, so he did as he was told. Bee walked over and kicked him in the face. "Shit," he whined in pain. She kicked him 3 more times.

"That's for putting your hands on my sister, pussy," she said.

"Man, y'all gone kill me?" he questioned.

"Shut the fuck up, you lucky I don't kill yo bitch ass," Bee said, kicking him once more. Black walked in the room and grabbed the last two bags before rushing out. Bee picked up the duffle bag on the bed and threw it over her shoulder, before putting the pistol to the back of his head. "Count to a 1,000, pussy. If you get up before we gone, and I see you, I'mma kill yo bitch ass." He started counting, showing he understood. She backed out the door making sure he didn't try anything. She opened the door and placed the pistol inside her bag and walked as fast as possible out the hotel. Once she made it outside, Black was waiting on her. Bee got in the passenger side and they pulled off.

"You cool girl?" Bee asked, once they were on the highway. Tears rolled down Black's face. Bee looked at her friend and regretted bringing her along for this roller coaster ride called the streets.

"I'm good," she said, wiping the tears from her eyes. "Did you kill that mutha fucker?" she asked while hitting the steering wheel.

"I couldn't, we on camera going in the room… but, believe me when I say I wanted to."

"I don't give a fuck, you should've killed him for putting his hands on me," Black yelled, her emotions getting the best of her. This wasn't good in the game they just entered. They needed to leave their emotions at home when running the streets. Bee was starting to think she'd got them in over their heads. She didn't know if they were ready to play at this level, if any level at all.

"And then what? We gone be on the news, wanted for murder. Huh you gotta think past go, remain calm, and don't show your emotions to these niggas. They already think we ain't ready, because we bitches. So, we gotta prove ourselves. What happened at that hotel can't happen again. You froze up and it could've been the end of our lives. This shit ain't no different from fighting these hoes at school. I need my ride or die bitch with me. I need that Black, if we gone do this. You need to remember that losing when those things come out, is not the same as losing a fight, it's our lives," Bee said, highly annoyed. Black looked over at her girl, she was right. She needed to get it together and hold Bee down like she always did for her. Acting weak could get them murdered, and she almost cost them their lives. She promised herself it wouldn't happen again. She was a fighter and had to be strong all her life. She learned from her mistakes and wouldn't make them again. The day that her parents died in a car crash, she'd lost it all. She went years without anyone caring about her until she met Bee. Bee was the sister she never had. From day one, Bee became a sister, parent, and teacher. She showed her everything from personal hygiene to using her looks to get what she wanted, and never once did she ask for anything in return, until now. Black planned to do better, because she knew better. She had to hold her friend down. No more mistakes like today.

"I'm sorry," Black said looking at Bee. Bee wouldn't look at her, she was a shame to call her a friend at the moment.

"Don't be, just don't let it happen again," she said firmly while looking out the window.

"Look Bee this my first time doing something like this, and you right, I did freeze up, but it won't happen again I promise," Black shot back nervously. Bee was insensitive because she had to be, she was doing this for Black's own good. If Black got off easy, mistakes like this would continue. Bee wanted to get paid, not lose her life. All it took was a split second for them to never breathe again. She had to be hard on Black cause she didn't wanna lose her.

"Oh really," Bee said mockingly. Black's heart started racing. Bee never talked down to her, this was her first time not believing in her. It hurt to hear the disappointment in her voice. She always talked to Black respectfully. Black looked over at her sister and friend and saw disappointment on her face. The rest of the ride was awkward. Bee stared out the window in deep thought. What was she doing getting in bed with the devil? She dated drug dealers and it never end well. One of two things always happened: they ended up in prison or dead. The path she was taking would more than likely end the same way, but she felt this was the only way after all they went through. They deserved a piece of the good life, even if it was only for a moment. Her life was always hard, so what difference did it make. She wanted enough money to do as she pleased, and if it was up to her, they'd have it one way or another. She was committed to the plan even though she wasn't confident, her girls were cut out to be hustlers. When they pulled in the driveway, Black cut off the engine.

"You still mad?" she asked, looking at Bee with a sad face.

"No, I wasn't really mad at you freezing up. I'm mad because for a moment I thought I might lose you. That little hesitation could've got one of us killed. I need you to always make the right decisions when pistols come out. Be willing to destroy any in everything that gets in our way. It's killed or be killed, that's the reality of the game," Bee explained. Black took a moment to sip on the tea. She was right and fighting with her was wrong. She'd take her lesson like a woman and learn from it.

"I'm sorry," she whispered, and Bee gave her a hug, giving up on her tough girl act.

"I'm sorry too, but I gotta go. So, jump yo yellow ass out," Bee said smiling.

"Ok," Black said with a slight giggle while getting out with the duffle bags. Black felt some type of way and she had to make it up to her another time.

Bee got in the driver seat, then saw the bag of money on the passenger side floor. She thought about running it inside, but she was already late. She pulled off on her way to meet Martez's fine ass to take care of business. After speeding, she arrived at his office. *"Shit,"* she thought, this was the second time she looked a hot mess coming to see him. She was wearing a black jumpsuit, looking like a tomboy. Bee reminded herself this was a business meeting. Even though she was underdressed, she still had sex appeal and swag on her side. Dressed down or not, any man would love to have her on his arms.

Bee entered the building and was greeted by security. "Hi Ms. Gomaz," she said and an upbeat pleasant voice. *Somebody got some dick last night,* Bee thought. "You can head back, Mr. Reynolds is waiting for you," she added, fixing her desk and giving a big smile.

"Thanks." Bee politely said before walking in his office. When she entered, she gazed around the room. His office was nice and clean, without any pictures of a family, so she guessed he was single.

"Hi Ms. Gomez," he said, reaching out to shake hands. When Bee looked into his eyes, her heart skipped a beat for the second time in as many meetings. She had to have him, even if it was only for a night. He was handsome. She never saw anything like him. Bee was always secure with her appearance because she was beautiful, but in this moment, she hoped he liked how she looked. "Hi Mr. Reynolds," she replied, shaking his hand. His touch was soft, and she felt faint.

"Have a seat," he instructed. She took a seat immediately. Something about him made her want to submit to him, and do anything, to please him. She was confused, because she liked to be the dominant one in the relationship. When she was around him, he was in control. "So, Ms. Gomez, I did my background check on you and one thing I've learn is you ain't the police."

"The police?" she said cutting him off and sitting up in her chair. "How you think I was the police?" she added, cocking her head back.

"I'm sorry if I offended you Ms. Gomez," he apologized. He then continued, "but you need to understand where I'm coming from. When you walked in my office, I didn't know that. I didn't know shit about ya," he said letting a little of the hood outta him. She sat quiet for a second, lost in his swag, which was off the charts. A man so desirable was enough to turn a queen into a fool. Being around him made her tremble, and tingles erupted inside her, creating a fire within. She knew it was wrong to lust over a man but couldn't help herself. She could imagine him lifting her on his desk and fucking her. This type of lust was new. Men were toys to play with as she willed, but she could see herself catching feelings for him. Bee pulled herself together.

"Ok let's move on, you called me here to tell me...?" she asked raising her eyebrow. He smiled and stared into her eyes. "I called this meeting to inform you that it'll cost 100,000 dollars to skip that line," he said licking his lips like LL Cool J. He knew he was every bitch's wet dream, and it showed in his confidence. Bee thought about the money they'd make off this club, so $100,000 was a small thing to pay to get things rolling. It took money to make money. They were investing in their future.

"So how do we go about doing this?" she questioned. Martez stood up and walked over to her. "How does a woman who just left a group home have $100,000 to skip a damn line?" he asked, folding his hands over his chest before saying, "If you don't mind me asking?" Bee looked at him before saying, "I do mine, but I'll answer if you answer a question for me first."

"What's that?" he replied.

"How does a murder become a lawyer?" she asked smiling slightly.

"Everything you read isn't true…. but I'll answer anyways. He must have good friends," he smirked. Then he stood over her and held his hand out to help her to her feet. He pulled her close enough that their bodies touched. She swallowed hard, feeling his strong chest against hers. "Just bring the money to me, I'll take care of the rest," he whispered, and his lips brushed her ear. Bee stepped back, and he smiled, noticing the effect he had on her.

"I'mma be right back," she said, before leaving his office as fast as possible. She grabbed the bag outta the car. She strolled back into his office and threw it on the desk.

"It's an extra $25,000 in there for you." Martez looked in the bag and laughed.

"My fee was included," he said.

"Well put it down as a retainer, I want you as my lawyer," she said, walking out the office like a boss.

(Meanwhile)

Tre Boi sat on the front porch at the spot on Normal smoking a blunt. He laughed at two kids on the corner fighting. Even tho they were only about 12 or 13 they looked like seasoned fighters. They move their heads avoiding the blows being thrown at them. He watched a little longer before deciding to break it up.

"A, that's enough." He yelled. They both glanced over and saw Tre Boi and reluctantly stopped. "What y'all out here fighting for any ways?" he asked while walking over to them.

"Man, he owe me a dollar and won't pay me," the taller one out of the two boys said. " I don't owe that nigga shit," the other one said, looking up at Tre Boi. "He said I could have that dollar," he continued.

"I ain't say you could have shit," the tall one yelled and threw a blow. Tre Boi stepped in the way, and it landed on his chest

"Look y'all lil nigga's need to fall the fuck back. Out here fighting over a dollar," he said. Tre Boi went and his pocket and pulled out 5 grand. He took out two hundred dollars and gave them both one. Their eyes lit up like they had won the lotto.

"Damn bro, good looking out," the tall one said smiling from ear to ear. "Look imma tell y'all once, I bet not see y'all out her clowning over no money. When you love yo nigga's you share with them...But also, a man keeps his word...When you tell someone you gone pay them back, that's what you do," he said, schooling them before walking away. He went back to the house and as always there was a party inside. There was woman from the hood bagging up dope. TDN was sitting on the couch getting head as some people looked on. "What good skud," TDN said while smiling at him.

"You on some other shit," Tre Boi said, laughing. TDN was live screening the whole thing as the woman sucked him like a porn star. Tre Boi was stunned at the show. He thought about getting his dick sucked as well but wasn't into the group sex shit. Crazy shit happened all the time. When you were the shit like they were, all the bitches wanted them. See, in Chicago, the hitta got most of the love. They were warriors and heroes in the hood. The kids looked up to them. The women wanted to fuck them, and the hoe ass nigga's wanted to be them. Life was good at the top. With Ryan out the game, he had the block to himself. Money was coming in like never before. Tre Boi walked in the back room and closed the door. He wanted some time alone, just to think. Tre Boi walked over and sat on the couch. June gave him the 100 bands, so he paid TDN and his little T.H.O.T bitch. He was thinking about using the cash to get a new car, and was contemplating whether to do it or not, but he really didn't need shit right now. When he thought about it, he had everything he wanted. There was a knock on the door before one of the thots walked in. He glanced up at the naked woman.

"Boi why you in here by yo self?" she asked

"Don't worry about it. Ain't no use in wasting conversation. I got what you came in here for," he said, pulling his pants down revealing his limed penis. "Boi you crazy," she said, walking over and sitting on the sofa next to him. Tre Boi looked at her like she lost her mind.

"Bitch you came in here to run yo mouth or get down. Like I said, I ain't try'na talk. I want yo mouth full," he said firm. The look on her face was priceless. She looked turned on and offended all at once. But it didn't stop her from dropping to her knees and licking his cock. She sucked him into her mouth and watched in amazement as it grew to full size. She pulled him out her mouth. "Damn you a grower. Yo shit getting big as hell," she said. He didn't respond, just grabbed the back of her head, putting his cock back in her mouth like the boss he was.

CHAPTER SIX

Two Days Later

*M*artez walked out his last business meeting heading to his car. After securing Ms.Gomaz license for her club. Over the last two days, he had meetings with 3 state employees, he paid them 25,00 each to get the job done. He hopped into his XT5, and thought about calling Ms.Gomaz, to reveal the good news. She was all he thought about since their meeting. He loved the way her smile lit up an entire room. He had no business thinking of her, in anyway other than a client. But every time he was around her, he found it hard to stay focus. He hoped he didn't cross that line. He needed to keep the business between them in perspective, because if they had any relations, business would end, once she learned he'd never give his heart to a woman. He broke hearts in millions of pieces, and didn't wanna be tied down, a relationship wasn't in his future. His focus was maintaining a successful career, anything besides that didn't matter. He was on his way to being the best defensive attorney in the state. A woman would only slow him down. He put all thoughts of Ms.Gomaz to the back of his mind, before pulling off. Martez picked up his iPhone and called one of his female friends, to get his dick wet. He wanted to remove any lustful thoughts before calling Ms.Gomaz in fear of what he might say.

(Meanwhile)

Bee hid in the bathroom holding her pretty savages in hand as Black sold the last 65 pounds. When she heard the door close, she walked out, guns in hand.

"Bitch you think you Bo-hanning," Black spoke while getting the duffle bag. "Fuck you," Bee said, tucking her guns under her arms inside a bag of money. After what happened last time, anytime they met a buyer they wore all black with hoodies on, and they ordered the room online with a stolen credit card that Glory provided off the dark web. When they entered the hotel, they used the back door with their hoodies on. Next time someone tried them, they'd find a body in the room. Black grabbed the money and they exited. Once inside the car, Bee's mind went to the person occupying it: Martez. She couldn't believe she was still thinking about him after two days. She was frustrated for letting a man occupy space in her mind. She wanted him cause everything about him felt like a mystery.

"What you over there thinking about?" Black asked, looking at the road.

"You don't even wanna know," Bee said, letting out a loud sigh.

"Whatever it is, you better snap outta it, you gotta go to Colorado and see what's up with Tez's connect," Black said. She was right. Bee had business to take care of, that's what she should've been focused on, not some man. No matter how fine he was. "I know girl, don't worry I'm good," Bee said, flashing a fake smile. Bee's phone rung, and when she looked at the screen, she saw it was the devil himself, Martez.

"Hello," she answered smiling from ear to ear.

"Hi, this is Mr. Reynolds. I'm calling to inform you that when you're ready to open your business you'll have your license." Just hearing his voice made her smile.

"Ok....... thanks Mr. Reynolds. I wanna meet with you, for help with paperwork for the club.," she lied.

"I'm a defense attorney, that's not the kind of work I do," he stated being polite.

"Oh, I'm so sorry," she said embarrassed. Her excuse to see him backfired.

"No apologies necessary, but don't bull shit me Ms. Gomaz. You don't need an excuse to see me, just ask me out," he joked. He saw through the games and could tell by how she looked at him, she had it bad. Before Bee knew what happened, the words came out.

"Would you like to go out sometime?"

"Damn that's a first for me Ms. Gomaz. I've never had a woman ask me out. But I got a question, is it a date or business? Because you didn't say," he asked giving her a hard time.

"A date," she said, rushing the words out before losing confidence to ask.

"It depends who's paying, because as a gentleman, I can't allow you to pay," he said, enjoying this little game they were playing.

"You can pay as long as I get to see you," Bee said, flirting back.

"Will you be picking me up?" he chuckled.

"No, you can pick me up tonight at 9, if it works for you?"

"Ya, that's cool, just text me the address."

"Oh, right, bye," she said, hanging up the phone. When she looked over, Black was all in her mouth. "Bitch who was that?" Black asked, parking the car in their driveway. "Bitch why you all in my tea?" Bee spat out the side of her mouth. Black was noisy. She always wanted to know everything going on in their lives.

"Come on Bee, who was it?" Black asked poking out her bottom lip like a baby.

"Bitch you just got to know everything."

"Mmm, hummm."

"If you must know it was Martez, we got a date tonight," Bee blushed.

"Bitch look at you blushing over a nigga. Let me find out you believe in love."

"You ain't gotta love to fuck," Bee said, sounding convincing. The truth was, she didn't know him on a personal level and she was already getting feelings she couldn't explain. She already liked him more than any man from her past. There was something about his smile, and the way he looked at her, like he was reading her mind, and knew what she was thinking. Bee wanted to get to know everything about him. When she saw him tonight, she'd be on point. Ya, she was going shopping A.S.A.P.

*****

Kia decided to end her trip to Africa early. She was healed and wanted to get back to the block and run her empire. She'd spent enough time giving, and even found new love. It was time to run it up and put the past behind her, she thought as she stepped off the private jet.

It felt good to be back in the States. A smile spread across her face just seeing her city. Milwaukee was home no matter how much of the world she experienced. She'd always feel comfortable here over any place.

After months in Africa her skin glowed, making her look even more beautiful.

The driver opened the car door for her as she let the wind blow through her hair. Kia got into the car and he closed the door behind her. She felt the leather against her back and relaxed. She hated leaving Danjunema in Africa, but he had business to attended to.

She planned to use the time away to get some money and some good dick.

It wasn't cheating if you didn't get caught. "Where to?" the driver asked. "Drive. Just drive around, I wanna see my city," she said while laying back. She stared out the window as he drove.

Kia loved this place with all her heart. She thought of new plans to take over but didn't know where to begin. Maybe she'd just stay away and get money in Madison. Her mind wandered to June and his business purpose, and whether she'd take him up on it. While in Africa, she thought about using him to take over Cash's empire but decided against it.

After riding around for a while, Kia realized that she no longer had a place to call home in Milwaukee. She'd lost her apartment months ago. Everything slipped her mind after losing Angel.

"Damn," she said out loud. She picked up her phone and called her husband.

"Hello beautiful," he said once he answered. Kia smiled just hearing his voice, it brought her joy now.

"Baby I just made it to Milwaukee, and I don't have a place to stay. Do you own any homes here?" she asked

"No, I don't. Why don't you stay in a hotel," he said.

"No, I don't want to daddy, where is our nearest house?" she asked. She'd already spent enough time in hotel rooms to last a few lifetimes. Now that she was the wife of a very powerful man, she wanted the best of everything. The world would be her playground.

"Chicago, hunny," Danjunema responded.

"OK daddy can you have somebody leave me a key?" she asked.

"I'll call the housekeeper and she'll let you in," he said. "Is that all, cause I'm in a very important meeting," he added.

"Oh, I'm sorry, text me the info so I can get there," she said.

"OK, bye, love you," he responded.

"Love you too," she said, hanging up the phone. A moment later she received the text with the address. Kia gave the driver the address and told him to take her there.

She laughed because she'd just returned home cause she was home sick, but she didn't even stay an hour. But that was the life of the rich and famous. She sat there deep in her thoughts until they pulled up to the house. Kia loved how her man was so rich that he had houses his wife had never visited before. She wondered how much he was worth as she stepped out the car and walked to the front door. A stunning beauty stood there, dressed in a maid uniform.

"Hi," the maid said. Kia wasn't in the mood to communicate with the help, so she walked past like she heard nothing.

She looked over her shoulder at the two vehicles in the driveway and saw her team of mercenaries.

She had all the protection in the world and today she felt like the President as they began to surround the house like the secret services. *"Having money was great,"* she thought, before asking the maid where the master bedroom was located.

"Follow me," she responded. Kia followed her to the master bedroom before dismissing her for the day. She didn't need her monitoring her movement cause tonight she planned to get fucked.

Kia began to undress to take a shower and wondered just what the night might bring. She smiled, hoping it brought her something big and thick.

(Later That Night)

Martez was really feeling himself as he drove to go get Bee. After talking to her, he changed into some all-white True Religion jeans, a white denim True Religion jacket, and Christion Louboutin shoes, which were white as well. He wore his favorite Carter watch. As he rode to his destination, he sang along to Future and Drake hit, "Diamonds Dancing." He pulled up on Raymond Rd. and turned the music down before calling Bee, informing her he was outside. When Bee walked out, he got out and opened the door. He couldn't take his eyes off her curvy frame. Her dress clung to her body so tight, he saw the imprint of her nipples and nipple rings through the fabric. Bee wasn't wearing a bra either, so they were on full display. In her hand, she held a jacket just in case the restaurant had a problem with her girls being out. Also on display, was her 2 sleeves of tattoos.

"Thank you," She said while nervously getting inside. Martez ran over and got into the driver seat before pulling off. "You look amazing," he said. Bee gave a shy smile before saying, "Thank you. You don't look bad yourself. She joked."

"What kind of music you like?" he asked, try'na make her comfortable.

"All kinds! Whatever you got in mind is fine," she replied. Martez knew they had a big age difference and didn't want to take it too far back on her. But love songs were his shit, so he played Maxwell's, "This Woman's Work."

"Oh, this that song from love and basketball. I can do this she said laying back in her seat. He smiled and pulled off. On their way out, they made small talk, but he saw she was nervous. She seemed on edge being alone with him. Bee was really feeling him and seeing him in street clothes instead of a suit gave her lustful urges. They arrived at Ruth Chris Steak House. Once again, he opened her door like a gentleman.

"Thanks."

"You don't have to thank me Ms. Gomez, this is what a man does for a lady."

"Please call me Bee. Ms. Gomez makes me feel old," she said sweetly.

"Bee, I like that," he said, as they made their way inside. Once they were seated, they placed their order."

"Do you mind if I ask you something?" Bee asked.

"What's on yo mind," he said, giving her his attention.

"What is a man as fine as you doing single?" she asked, staring in his eyes.

"Who said I was single?" he said. Bee scrunched up her forehead, then looked him up and down with disgust. Martez laughed at the facial expression.

"Nah I'm bullshitting with you," he said. Bee took a deep breath. "But next time, ask a person if they single or not before you ask them out," he teased. Bee shot him the evil eye and mouthed "Shut up" and they shared a laugh. "But for real, I'm single because I haven't found a woman who can handle my lifestyle," he stated.

"And what kind of lifestyle is that?"

"Well I need a woman to understand, I don't want a relationship I want relations," he confessed without taking his eyes off her. Bee licked her lips seductively. His straight forwardness turned her on. She'd met guys who only wanted sex but lied and told her everything but the truth. She respected this about him. At least he wasn't selling her dreams or a happily ever after.

'So, what you looking for is a women to fuck from time to time?'

"More or less," he said. It felt like she'd met her dream lover, she wasn't the girl who wanted a fairy tale love story. In front of her sat a man who genuinely wanted the same thing. Most men start out only wanting some pussy but end up wanting a relationship.

"Ok I wanna know if we fucked and one of us didn't like it, it's cool if we never try it again? You ain't gone blow my line up if you get some good pussy?" Bee questioned looking into his eyes. Martez stared back.

"Ya that's fine with me, but I'm sure you'll be asking for more," he said confidently.

"So, what we doing here?" she asked.

"We're on a date," he said, not comprehending what she was getting at.

"Dates are for people who want relationships. What we need to be is a hotel," she said, standing up to leave. Martez understood that without a problem. He placed 200 dollars on the table for a meal they wouldn't eat and followed her out.

20 minutes later they walked into a room and Bee was all over him. She'd wanted this moment since laying eyes on him. Her fantasy was coming true. He slid his hand up her skirt, caressing her thighs. His finger toyed with her clit. Bee wasn't in the mood to make love, what she'd come to do was fuck! She began to run her hands up and down the length of his dick, and just like she figured, he had a big one. She'd had enough of the touching and wanted to see it.

She unzipped his jeans and pulled out his 9inch cock. She was having an outta body experience. All the things she'd done in the last hour wasn't who she was. Bee wasn't a hoe, but she'd also never wanted a man this much. She found herself on the floor with his dick dangling in front of her. As she looked at his cock, thoughts of never giving head on the first date came to mind, but it wasn't a date, and something about today was different. She wanted to show him everything she had to offer sexually.

Bee took him in her mouth and sucked on the head and jagged it with two hands.

"Damn ma," he said, placing his hand on the back of her head. She licked him up and down while massaging his balls with the other hand. He had a huge grin on his face. Bee looked at him smiling before deep throating his dick. She got all but two inches. He pulled her up, bent her over the bed before rubbing his dick up and down her pussy. "Put it in," Bee said. She never thought she'd be this turned on by anyone. She was so wet he slid in with one powerful stroke. She thought he'd be rough like most boys, but he surprised her with a slow stroke that gave her so much pleasure without the pain, and took her to places she never thought possible. He was hitting the bottom of her pussy. If she didn't know better, she would've thought he was making love to her, passionate love.

"I'm cumming," she yelled, cumming for the first time in her life. Martez didn't respond verbally, but he did pick up the pace. Bee came all over him not once but twice, before he pulled out nutting on the floor. Martez laid on the bed as she went to take a shower basking in the glory of their sex. Her sprit hasn't been this high an awhile. She'd just had the best sex of her life. There wasn't a man who came close to making her feel how he had. Martez made her cum twice within an hour. He wasn't the relationship type, but neither was she, or at least she hoped she wasn't. At that moment, she second guessed herself. No, tonight was just sex, no matter how good it was, no feelings, whatsoever. After her shower she found Martez sleeping. She grabbed her clothes and got dressed before leaving. Bee called a cab and went home.

(Meanwhile)

A group of teenage boys & girls sat on a porch in Chicago, smoking and drinking. Anywhere else they would've been home sleeping for school in the morning but not on Lamron. They were the lost souls no one believed in.

"Man look, Chief Keef is the best thing out the city. If it wasn't for him, none of these niggas would have deals, fuck is you niggaz talking about," one of the boys yelled, try'na get his point across.

The girls just shook their heads, tired of hearing his argument. It had been a debate in the city since GBE & OTF gained fame in 2011. It was a broken record to the young lady who wasn't interested. While they were too busy debating, just up the block in the gangway a group of 5 men wearing all black were creeping up on them. They were there to revenge the murder of Big G. Normally they wouldn't kill children, but their order was to murder anyone in sight. Laughter could be heard as they approached guns ready to commit mass murder. The first one spent the corner, and he saw the kids, but it didn't stop him from firing his weapon.

Bloc! Bloc! Bloc! Boc! Boc! Boc!

The rest of them opened fire on the children. They fired over a hundred shots before walking up and putting a round into each of their heads. When their getaway car pulled up, they casually walked to it before getting in. The gun shots woke Tre Boi from his sleep. They seemed to go on forever. When they finally stopped, he knew somebody lost their life. *"Damn,"* he thought while getting off the couch and going in the front room, which was filled with naked women who seemed to be deaf, cause they were still sleeping after the gun shots. He looked out the window police were everywhere. When he noticed them at the kids hang out his heart dropped. Something inside him told him that whatever happened was meant for them. He got up and went to have a drink, unable to go back to sleep.

(An Hour Later)

Kia stepped out the car wearing a Gucci dress and heels. She was on a mission to get fucked, so she wasn't wearing any panties. Her ass giggled with every step she took.

When she walked up to the bar all eyes were on her. She went inside while her driver waited in the parking lot. Not long after taking a seat at the bar, she spotted him, the lucky man who'd have a chance to be on the receiving end of her goodies. His waves and dark skin were attractive to her. He had just the right amount of thug to go along with his good looks.

She'd be surprised if he was alone. So, she decided to order a drink before she approach him.

She ordered a double shot and watched as the bartender poured her drink. Kia gave him a twenty-dollar bill and told him to keep the change. When she glanced up, he was still sitting alone. He looked to be in deep thought about something, and Kia began to wonder what was on his mind.

He looked up and they stared into each other's eyes a moment. She gave him a shy smile, which he returned before standing up and walking over to her.

Kia's heartbeat began to speed up at the thought of what she was about to do.

"Hi, is this seat taking?" he asked. Kia gave cheating one more thought. She knew it was wrong and hated it when it happened to her. But she needed someone that could go deep inside her, someone who could hit the spots her husband couldn't.

"No!" she responded, throwing caution to the wind and deciding to go through with her plans.

"Mind if I have a seat?" he asked.

"No, I don't mind," she shyly said putting on an act.

"My name is Tre Boi, it's nice to meet you," he said, putting out his hand to shake. Kia shook his hand before saying, "I'm Kia...and it has yet to be determined if it's nice to me you."

Tre Boi smiled, wondering if she meant what he thought.

Kia licked her lips seductively, hoping he understood.

"It'll be a pleasure," he replied, and they shared a laugh, both seeming conformable with where the night was heading. He saw the lust in her eyes across the room. The moment he approached he knew he was fucking. He stared at the older woman and wondered if the saying, "it gets greater later," was true before taking a seat.

"What you doing drinking alone?" he asked, looking into her eyes. Kia held eye contact before saying, "My husband is in Africa, and I'm enjoying my time alone," she said before placing her drink to her lips and sipping from it.

"Damn it's like that? You gotta wait until he gone to enjoy yourself?" he questioned. Kia placed her drink down on the counter.

"Nah, I enjoy myself with him when he around, just not doing what I'm here looking for," she said raising her eyebrows.

"And what's that?" Tre Boi asked, sure he already knew.

Kia stood up, leaned close, and whispered in his ear, "sex!" she said rubbing her hand up his leg. "I want to enjoy a big dick while he gone. You think you can help me with that?" she added, placing her hand on his cock as it grew to full size. Tre Boi watched her eyes get wide as she felt him.

He smirked before saying, "You tell me, is the dick big enough to enjoy?" he asked.

His cockiness made Kia smile inside. "Just cause it's big don't mean I'll enjoy it boi. You gotta know how to use it," she said before sitting down and fanning herself to cool down.

Tre Boi laughed at the effect he was having on her. The bartender strolled past them and Tre Boi ordered them a round of drinks. When he went to retrieve them, they picked the conversation up where they left off. "We'll enjoy a few drinks, then I'll change the world for you...Once I'm done, you'll never look at sex the same," he said, feeling his self as his drinks kicked in.

"We'll see," Kia responded, looking forward to feeling him inside her.

"So why we here? Why don't you tell me a little about yourself?" she asked.

"Ain't much to know! I'm from the hood and Chicago, and I'm in the streets, never worked a day in my life. At any moment, I could be dead or in jail. I'm not looking for a woman, and I see you ain't looking for a man. If we fuck that's all that's gone come from it," he said, being brutally honest with her. Kia smiled, loving that he understood what she wanted and knew what he wanted as well.

"How bout you?" he asked.

"I'm from Milwaukee! That's all you need to know for the night, and don't worry, I don't want nothing but dick," she said giving him a matter fact look. "Fuck me good tonight, and I might change yo life boi," she added. Tre Boi frowned his face up at her comment. "Who the fuck you think you talking to shorty? Ain't shit you can do to change my life that I can't do on my own!" he said putting her in her place.

He wasn't the type of man to have a woman believing he needed them. He stood on them, and that's what he planned on doing tonight.

Tre Boi knew her type, and a woman like her needed to be handled roughly. It would turn her on more than she would be able to understand.

Kia was lost for words and turned on all at once. She was a boss bitch, and it's been a while since anyone talked to her like that.

"You know what how much money in yo bag?" he asked.

Kia skewed her face up at the question. "Why the fuck you asked that?" she answered, a little offended.

Tre Boi stood to his feet and put his hand under her skirt, then rubbed her pussy. The moment he touched it, he knew she enjoyed the way he was handling her. *"Ya she was the type who wanted it rough, "*he thought.

"I'm asking the questions," he said and kept rubbing her clit. She took a deep breath before responding, "30 thousand," she said closing her eyes while letting out a soft moan. Tre Boi was shocked at the amount she was carrying. It turned him on more, maybe she wasn't lying when she said she could change his life.

"You want to know why I asked?" he questioned.

Kia shook her head, unable to speak. "Cause you gone pay for the dick tonight!" he said.

Kia opened her eyes at the sound of their drinks being placed on the table. The bartender looked at them suspiciously before walking away. Tre Boi placed a finger inside her as she was about to speak, stopping her in her tracks. "This ain't up for debate, you either pay or I leave," he said in a confident tone that brought her to a climax. Unable to hold her moans, she let out a scream which brought the attention of everyone in the bar to them. "Okay, okay, I'll pay," she said staring into his eyes as she came down from her climax. He smirked. "Then get yourself together and let's get the fuck outta here," he said, picking up his shot and downing it, before walking out and leaving her to pay the bill. She watched as he left before looking around at everyone staring at her and blushed.

******

30 minutes later, Kia unlocked the hotel door. She was beginning to feel guilty for cheating on her husband. But he

couldn't provide what she craved. The moment the door opened, Tre Boi picked her up from behind and carried her inside placing her face down on the bed. She slowly rolled over once she felt him step away. When she turned around, he stood there with his hand out.

"Before we go any further, I need my money up front," he said seriously. Kia smiled, loving the idea of paying for sex like she had a pimp. There was something so sexy about doing what others wouldn't that drove her crazy. It lit a fire inside her. She reached inside her bag and pulled out the whole $30,000.

"Is this enough?" she asked, throwing it to him. Tre Boi caught the stack of bills and smirked. He wondered what she did for a living to pay him 30 bands like it was nothing.

"Ya, it'll do," he said thumbing through the bills, before placing them on the nightstand.

"So now that's out the way, can I get what I'm owed?" Kia asked, sitting up in bed. Tre Boi stepped back and began to undress. When he was naked, Kia was amazed at what stood before her. She watched as he stroked himself to full hardness. He asked if this was what she needed. She moaned as he moved her. Sitting on the bed, she only had to lean forward to suck his cock. She sucked for a moment only out of habit, before pulling away and undressing herself. She looked at his dick which seemed to grow even harder with her attention. Kia laid back on the bed with her ass at the edge and her legs hanging over. Tre Boi picked up her legs and placed her feet on his shoulder as he stood in front of her. He took his dick and rubbed it up and down her clit, between her lips, and her swollen and sensitive clitoris. Kia went crazy just thinking about the pleasure to come as she moaned up a storm waiting for him to enter her. She screamed in pleasure as the first four inches disappeared inside her. He paused for a brief second before slowly moving onwards.

Kia started to slowly grind herself against him, before yelling for him to fuck her.

"Ooooh my goddd, you feel so good," she moaned at the feeling of how deep inside her he was.

"Tre Boi held her legs wide apart as he stroked deep and steadily. "Damn," he said loving how tight she was. *She felt like a virgin,* he thought.

"I know its good ain't it," she asked, once she saw the look on his face. He didn't answer, instead he stared down at her pussy lips tugging at him with each stroke. Kia reached down and rubbed the part of his cock too long to fit inside her as he continued to fuck her. She thanked God for the amazing climax building inside her as Tre Boi showed no sign of letting up in the near future.

CHAPTER SEVEN

Two Days Later

*B*ee landed in Colorado. But before leaving, she called and notified Ryan to set up a meeting. He sent a car to the airport for her. The moment she stepped outside, a driver rushed over and took her bags. He opened the limousine door and she got inside. After loading her bags, he pulled off. Bee sat in the back, reflecting on the wonderful night with Martez. Even though the sex was good, she hadn't called him and didn't plan to. It was a one-night stand...a good one, but still one and done. She gave him what he wanted, and he did the same. She told herself over and over again that she wasn't gone let dick drive her crazy. But here she was days later, still thinking about it. She knew the game and men too well. Guys like Martez couldn't take rejection, they were used to women chasing them. His ego would make him wonder why she never called. Once that happened, it was only a matter of time before he called her. And once that happened, he was hers. She was playing the waiting game, giving him enough time to wonder whether he put it down like he thought. She tried focusing on business. She was on her way to make a deal of a lifetime, a deal that could change her life forever. If Ryan did business with her, their years of hurting were behind them, and the sky was the limit. It was happening so fast, but they'd handle it. Bee was quick on her feet and always ahead of the game. She was always planning and thinking a few moves ahead of the rest. She thought about how they'd been hustling so hard and hadn't enjoyed the money. When she got home, she planned to spend a little something. They pulled up to a small white house. It was a nice home, but not what she expected. She thought he'd live in a mansion. The driver stepped out and opened her door.

"Follow me," he instructed, and she followed him inside the home. He gestured for her to walk ahead. The house was empty inside. There was nothing but plastic on the floors and ceilings and even on the walls. She walked in what she believed was the dining room, and saw Ryan sitting in front of the fireplace, his back facing them. She was nervous. Her body said something wasn't right about this place, and she wished she had her pretty savages.

"So Tez is dead?" Ryan asked, his deep voice coming alive. "He was a good friend of mines, and an even better business partner," he added with his back still facing her. She felt cold steel press against the back of her head as the driver held her at gun point. Bee waited to hear a loud bang, which meant she would never feel again, date again, or hug her friends again. She waited for it all to end. But Ryan voice replaced the loud bang.

"I use this house for executions only, but I'll give you two minutes to tell me why this room shouldn't be the last thing you see," he said, turning to look at her for the first time. When he saw her again, he remembered how much lust he had for this woman. It all came back to him; that night she was all he thought about. But this was business, it wasn't personal. She was scared to death but didn't let it show. She remained calm and cool with her poker face on. She wasn't scared of dying, if god come for her, then it must've been her time.

"Because I'm worth more alive than dead," she said with a smile on her face.

"Is this funny?" Ryan stood up yelling. The driver pushed her head forward and pressed the pistol harder against her. He was waiting for the go ahead and he'd blow her brains out. Bee took a second before speaking again. "Nah, but if I'm gone die, I ain't begging for my life if that's what you expect. I'mma hold my head high as if my nose bleeding," she said, sounding tough. But on the inside, she was hoping and praying it didn't end here. Ryan stared into her eyes and looked for a sign of weakness but saw none. He walked over to her and grabbed her face with both hands without breaking eye contact. "You're one hell of a lady if you're willing to stare death in the eyes without blinking," he said to Bee. "Put the gun away," he told the driver. "I'mma give you a chance to prove why you're worth more alive than dead," Ryan said while walking back to his seat. The driver removed the pistols and Bee let out a deep breath, before saying, "I don't know if you know this, but Tez was robbed."

"How do I know you don't have anything to do with this," he said, cutting her off. "I guess you will never know! But like I was saying, when he was robbed, they took everything," she lied. Ryan shook his head and threw his hands in the air. "What does this have to do with me?"

"They didn't take the phone, so I have all his clientele. I was hoping to do business with you, but the problem is, I don't have money."

He was interested now. He was hurt about losing Tez as a friend. But that didn't compare to the pain he felt for losing his business. If she had his clientele, she was an asset, and was worth keeping alive. He believed in B.O.F. (business over friendship).

"You have all his clientele?" he questioned.

"Yes!"

"So how many pounds do you think you can handle a month?"

"2 hundred," she said, holding up two fingers. He stood up, walked over to her and grabbed her face. Then, he kissed her lips.

"We have a deal. I will have 2 hundred pounds delivered to you as soon as possible. All I need is an address." Bee was so happy, that she didn't even mind him kissing her without permission. She shook his hand and said she'd call with the address once she made it home. She needed to find a place for the delivery. They went over the prices of the pounds before his driver dropped her off at her hotel suite.

*****

Once safely inside her hotel room. She went straight to the shower and ran a hot bath. After almost dying, she just wanted to relax. She was relieved that Ryan would front her the pounds. Now she could use the $500,000 they had to open the club. She didn't want to run a hole in the wall club, no! They wanted the best of everything from this moment on. When she made it back to Madison, she planned to get a real-estate agent to find a building in the right location. Bee got undressed and stepped into the bathtub. Besides almost getting her brains blown out, life was great since entering the game. She went over her plans in her mind. They'd sell pounds off the line until the club was up and running. When everything was in motion, they'd slowly stop moving weight and hustle out the club. She wanted to prove that a woman was worthy of doing business at this level, so she planned to sell the pounds fast as possible. They were about to take over the Midwest. A powerful feeling washed over her as she laid in the hot water, a feeling she never experienced before. It was the power of knowing she controlled her own destiny. Bee wouldn't let anything in this world stand in her way.

(Chicago)

Martez pulled up to a warehouse on Chicago's eastside in a 2008 Chevy Impala. He was coming to meet Cash, one of the famous twins. Everybody in Wisconsin knew Money & Cash for pushing dope on a major level. He was here to conduct business. Once every 6 months they met at this spot. Inside the truck was 200 keys of cocaine in a hidden compartment. The warehouse door opened, and he pulled inside. He parked behind 3 black escalades before stepping out. He hated doing business with Cash, he was to flamboyant. It was a fed case waiting to happen. The only reason Cash wasn't doing life was his team of young savages that held things down. When they got jammed for bodies or drug charges, they never told. He was lucky not to have a rat nigga around him. In his circle, disloyalty was intolerable, and they lived by the code.

Martez looked at Cash in the corner of the room sitting at the table counting money and wearing all white Gucci from head to toe. What immediately attracted his attention was his diamond earrings and the B.O.M. charm with VS1 lighting up the room with the slightest movement. This was the reason he hated meeting him. They were making a drug transaction, they weren't at the NBA All-Star game. He didn't have a problem with how Cash dressed on his own time, but when conducting business, you should dress accordingly.

"What's good bro!" Cash yelled, throwing his hands in the air.

"You already know, business," Martez said. He wasn't into the gang thing anymore, but something inside him couldn't confess this to the guys. He didn't care what they thought, he just couldn't bring himself to say it out loud.

"I know you try'na get in and out college boy. The money in the same place as always. Oh, and tell Reese I said love the next time you see him."

"I got it skud, but no bullshit, you need to go visit bro," Martez said, taking a seat.

"Nah going to them joints ain't my style, hell no, that shit bad luck," Cash said, picking up a stack of money. "You go visit a nigga, the next thing you know, y'all in that bitch together," he added. Martez looked him up and down like he had just said the stupidest shit in the world.

"Skud you sound crazy as hell, nigga, I'm up there at least once a month, and I ain't never been to jail," he said heatedly. He hated hearing niggas use that argument, as an excuse for getting outta seeing their guy. If they were worried about jail, they'd put the drugs and guns down. Cash was a selfish nigga, always was. Ever since they were kids, he'd been looking out for himself. If it wasn't for Reese, Martez would've stopped doing business with him. It was his plug that paved the road leading to Cash kingdom. Without his connect, Cash wouldn't be shit. But you couldn't tell him that. As he put it, he was self-made. At times, Martez thought Cash believed he was King David born again. He was a great leader, but he couldn't bring the team together, and that alone made him inferior to their falling king.

"What's crazy about it?" Cash asked, staring into his eyes while try'na intimidate him. He didn't back down and held eye contact.

"What's crazy is that bro been down all these years and you wanna use superstition as your reason for not visiting."

"Ya whatever college boi, my beliefs are my beliefs. I ain't gone change who I am for no nigga," Cash said. They stared a few more seconds. "Everybody ain't got Reese to hold they hand or do a bid for them," Cash added, obviously annoyed. He didn't like Martez testing him like he was sweet. And on top of that, he felt Reese was crazy as hell for taking that case. If it was him, Martez would've done his own time like a man. But Reese was protective of him. Since childhood, Reese told Martez the streets weren't for him. He said he had potential. Cash was jealous of their big homie's favoritism. Reese didn't have a problem with the rest of them running the streets. It made Cash feel that Reese was saying they ain't have potential. Cash didn't understand how easy life was for Martez. In his eyes, everything always went right for him. Not only was he good looking and smart, but what really made Cash envy him was how he fell into a plug that was out of this world. Cash spent years try'na get the plug outta him. But Martez wouldn't let it happen. He always told Cash that the connect only wanted to do business with him.

"I'm outta here," Martez said, reaching out to shake up. Cash stared at his hand and mugged him before shaking up.

"Ya do that college boy," he said after they released each other's hands. Martez turned to leave before things got outta hand. It took a lotta will power to walk away. There was so much he wanted to say and do to Cash at the moment. But he'd be the bigger person and walk away, at least this time. One of Cash's men hopped in the impala to let him out. The money was in the same place, the last escalade. Once inside, he threw the escalade in reverse and backed out. As he pulled out the lot, he turned up the music and made his way home with 5 million in cash inside the hidden compartment. His mind all over the place. He hated how niggas played Reese once he went away. Reese always showed love to them in different ways. He held them down, showed them how to use a pistol, and for even more of them, he showed them how to get that bag. Niggas forgot him the moment he went away, but not Martez! Even if Reese hadn't taken that bid for him, he would've been there. His loyalty was deeper than the ocean. They were brothers, and he was his brother's keeper. They didn't share the same blood, but they had family ties. The things Cash said were true, Reese took that time outta love for him. But his debt to Reese was almost paid in full. He gave Reese a million in drug money 5 years ago, and paid for anything he wanted, and when he came home, he planned to give him a few more million. He laughed thinking of the first few years of Reese bid. It was rough. He was still a college student barely getting by. He sent money whenever he could, but only $20 or $30 at a time. Reese always appreciated it. Not once did he regret his decision. He told Martez not to worry about him all the time. Reese was only 4 years older than him, but the streets grew him up fast. He was the only big brother he ever knew. They'd known each other their whole life. Martez grew up next door to Reese in a foster home. When he was a child, everyone picked on him for being a "pretty boy," until Reese showed him how to fight, which he picked up fast. It wasn't long before he was putting hands on everyone his age. He pulled up to his house. Once he parked, he hit the bright lights 3 times and the brakes 6 times, before putting the left turn signal on to open the compartment. He got out and grabbed the 2 duffle bags hiding inside. His 10,000 square foot mansion was mesmerizing. It had 10-foot high double doors, a grand staircase, music room, a formal study, an exercise studio, and a theater. There was also a separate wing on the first floor. The master suite featured an elaborate vestibule entrance, a sumptuous appointed bedroom, along with a walk-in closet. His house was lovely, he thought as he entered the living room and took a seat on his white leather sectional while setting the bags on the marble table. He didn't need to count it. Cash was great with making sure the money was correct. Every 6 months he made 1 million playing middleman between his Mexican connect and Cash. Cash was the only person he did business with. At that time, Cash came across $250,000 from his twin brother, Money, who was locked up. Cash spent the whole $250,000 with him, and the rest was history. He got the keys on consignment for $20,000 a key and sold them to Cash at $25,000. At this time, keys sold for anywhere between $35,000 to $42,000. Cash never complained cause he made more than enough to cash out. Martez sat back and thought about the day his life changed...

He was fresh outta law school and had just won his first big case. He got a young Mexican from Cali, who been visiting Madison, off on a homicide. A week after winning the trial, an old Mexican man entered his office to thank him for defending his nephew. Martez recognized him instantly as a high-ranking member of the Mexican cartel. He wasn't El Chapo by any means, but he was a boss in his own right. He recognized him from a wanted picture he saw while watching the Mexican news, which he watched because that's where the real killings happened. It was a state run by criminals. Chicago hoods ain't have shit on them. The older Mexican told him his name was Jose. He told Martez if he needed anything, to give him a call. Then he handed him a duffle bag with a hundred G's inside. Martez went home that night and thought about the life changing opportunity that walked into his office. He'd spent his whole life try'na stay away from the game. But this type of shit only happens in movies. Martez thought about Reese spending time in the justice system to keep him away from the lifestyle, he was thinking about getting into. He was grateful for his sacrifice but needed some extra cash. Most of his time as a lawyer was spent try'na get his friends out. He couldn't pick up cases, so he was only getting by. He hadn't made a name for himself, and really needed the money. He thought he would only do it a "few" times. The following morning, he called Jose and set up a meeting at Gloria's, a Mexican restaurant. They talked business and made a deal. Martez spent the $100,000 on 5 keys and sold them to Cash, who liked it so much that he placed an order a few days later for 10 more.

He got up and went to his bedroom to lay down. His thoughts brought him to Bee, and he wondered why she hadn't called. He knew she loved what he'd done to her. The body never lies, and she was cumming all over his dick. Nah, the sex wasn't the problem, she was playing hard to get. It was either that, or she thought there wasn't a future for them. Some women thought they knew what they wanted, and even though they didn't want a relationship, once good dick got involved, they couldn't make up their mind. Some ran away and never looked back. They were afraid and ashamed of opening their legs to someone who didn't want their heart. He understood it, and if he had a sister, he wouldn't want her used the way he used women. But Bee didn't seem like that kind of woman. She seemed strong in deceiving, at making decisions. Martez laughed, she was playing games with him, and it was working. She was a different type of woman, one he wanted to get to know.

(Meanwhile)

When Tre Boi got the news of the 7 murders the other night, he was devastated. It hit close to home because one of those killed was the tall kid, Boi Boi, who he had given the hundred dollars to.

The next day, he saw all their young faces on the news. The oldest was only 14. Tre Boi wasn't but 5 years older than them, but in hood years that was a lifetime. He looked over at TDN as they walked up the opps block searching for a victim. They held their AK47s like soldiers in Iraq ready for war. He was upset because this was the 3rd hood they went through tonight that was empty. Tre Boi was hot for revenge; he went hunting even after June told him not to. Cash gave orders to wait for more information before making a move. But he had all the information he needed, which was interesting. Why would the opps let Big G's murder go unpunished? If he was them, he wouldn't. So that's why they were there at the moment.

"Man, ain't nobody out here," TDN whispered before lowering his weapon. Just as Tre Boi was about to lower his, shots rang out.

Boc!boc! Boc!boc!

They ducked as the shots went past their heads. When TDN looked up, he saw the flame jumping off a firearm about half a block ahead of them. Once he located the source of the shots, he returned fired. His AK with a bonk stick released ripped rounds, overwhelming their opposition. Tre Boi joined him, turning the block into a Middle Eastern battlefield. They emptied their weapons before turning to run away. When they got in the getaway car, Tre Boi was upset.

"Damn we ain't even hit shit," he yelled.

"Speak for yoself nigga, I gotta body," TDN said pulling off. Tre Boi smacked his lips.

"Nigga you ain't hit shit, cause if you did, why you keep shooting?"

"I hit him with the first two.... watched him drop in all. The rest I let off to see if this bitch was gone jam," he said confidently. "Now that that's done, let's hit them hoes up that we met downtown the other day," he continued. "Nah fuck that, I'm try'na hit a few more of these niggaz blocks tonight," Tre Boi said, his thirst for blood unquenched.

CHAPTER EIGHT

3 Days Later

*B*ee touched down in Madison 2 days ago and set up the meeting to grab the pounds on the eastside. Today she was picking up the load. She sent a group text saying she was back in business. Orders came in before she left the house. *Damn this bitch be smacking,* she thought about the line before hopping in her car and pulling off. It didn't take long to pick up the truck with the pounds and make it back home safely. Black helped unload before they went out to breakfast. Once they were seated and had their food, Glory said, "I have been looking for a building with the perfect location, and I've found one." It was an abandoned warehouse on East Washington.

"I don't know girl," Bee said glancing at the building. It looked like a horror house. Some windows were missing, and it appeared like no one had stepped foot on the property in 20 years. "It's a nice location but the building looks like shit," she continued.

"Let me see," Black said taking the phone. "It's a little fucked up, but I like it," she said.

"Then it's done. If y'all like it, I love it," Bee said, reaching in her clutch to grab her vibrating phone.

"Hello," she answered. "Who is this?" Bee asked, knowing it was Martez.

"That's how you play the kid?" he questioned.

"What you mean that's how I'mma play you?" she asked, pretending to be bored with the conversation.

"Cut the bullshit girl, I'm try'na see you tonight and I ain't try'na play games. I'm not one of your lil boyfriends," he said, cutting her down to size real quick. Bee was turned on by how he talked to her. He acted like he owned her, and his confidence alone turned her on. "Where at?" she replied in a soft submissive voice, rubbing her legs together while putting pressure on her pussy. She rolled her eyes once she saw Glory and Black in her mouth. Bee screwed her face up at them in a way that said, "mind y'all own business." They knew it was a man without her saying a word because her body language said it all. From the moment she picked up the phone she'd been smiling like a schoolgirl with a crush.

"I'll come pick you up tonight," he said, loving how quickly she stopped playing games. He wanted her bad and he knew she wanted the same thing.

"Ok just call me an hour before you come."

"Ok bye," he said, and they hung up. The moment she got off the phone, Glory and Black asked, "Who was that?" Glory raised her eyebrows and Bee put her head down, feeling ashamed.

"Martez," she said, unable to hold her smile. Glory's mouth fell open.

"The lawyer?" she asked, as if they knew another one.

"Who the fuck is Martez?" Black spat out. Glory looked at Black like she had lost her mind.

"Bitch do you ever listen?" Glory asked.

"Ya, but only when y'all talking about something I wanna hear." She stressed the word "hear."

"Martez is our lawyer and a murderer," Glory said, looking at Bee like she was crazy for dating him. Instantly, Bee feelings were hurt by how Glory used the murder Martez might've committed against him. If she condemned him for what he might've done, then she for sure condemned Bee for the murders they knew she committed. If Glory looked down on him, she had to look down on her as well. Just the thought of her friend casting stones made tears come to her eyes. "Well so am I," Bee snapped. "Does that make me a bad person? Huh, does it? Does it make you look down on me as well?" Glory regretted what she said instantly when she saw tears running down her face.

"No... no, I didn't mean it how I said it. It didn't come out right. I would never judge you," Glory said, taking Bee's hands and tearing up as well. She would never judge the person that showed her so much, loved her when no one else would, and held her whenever she felt alone. Bee was her sister and she'd never look down on her. Bee saw the sincerity in her eyes. She wiped the tears, before giving them a shy smile. She pretended they were cool, even though she was still upset. "You bitches doing the most with these emotional ass moments," Black joked, and they shared a laugh.

"No but really, I'm sorry for judging you. I really didn't mean it like it came out."

"I know, don't worry about it."

"I gotta know more about the man that's taking my sister on a date, because I ain't never seen you smile like that with nobody," Black said, switching the topic.

Bee and Glory filled her in on information they'd share with her before, while she tuned them out. But now they had her full attention. Bee shared with them the night of passion, and how good it was. "Stop it. You fucked him on the first night? Hell no, not you bitch, you the biggest tease I know. You gotta really, really like him to give the pussy up that fast," Black said, staring at her. But once Bee didn't deny it, she asked, "You do?" Bee smiled, "I think I do girl."

(Later That Night)

Martez pulled up on Raymond Road and parked. He listened to Future's song, "No matter what."

"Your face your shape and the little things about you had the kid all in. Anytime we spend time, we spend more than we spend benjamin's. But the fuck this high siddity girl want to do with an astronaut kid. I'm asking myself questions, I had to understand...."

Future's song continued to play as Bee walked out, taking his breath away. She was killing it in a white dress that hugged her body. The dress could've been painted on. He stepped out, swag turned up, and opened her door. She thanked him before getting inside.

He stole a glance at her fat ass as she got inside. The moment he got inside she asked, "What hotel we going to?"

"Damn ma, you on business," he joked and pulled off.

"You said you ain't try'na play games, and neither am I."

"I ain't never playing games ma, I was just hoping to grab something to eat," he smiled, anticipating a smart remark.

"I think that sounds like a date." Bee said, playfully rolling her eyes. He laughed. "We don't have to call it that."

"Boy you crazy, we can call it what you want, but it's still a date," she said. Martez looked over and saw her smile. It was just as beautiful as her. There was something different about her. She didn't seem inconsiderate like most women. She had no objection with being friends, and she wasn't pushing a relationship on him. After they fucked, she didn't even call him. The 17-year age difference didn't seem to matter because she was mentally more mature than most women his age. He respected her because like him, she knew where she was headed. She had ambition, and at 18 years old, she had plans to become a business owner. She appeared independent. Martez glanced at her; she might be a blessing in disguise.

Once he stared a moment too long, Bee said, "Boy keep yo eyes on the road." Her words brought him outta his thoughts; she laughed, and he glanced at her. "What's funny?" he questioned. She turned in her seat and placed her shoulder on it. She didn't respond to his question, just stared at him, biting her lip sexually. Martez glanced over again. "What you staring at?" he asked, worried something was on his face.

"See, it don't feel good when it's done to you, so don't stare at people without saying something," she said. He laughed at how she was scolding him like a child.

"You got that," he said.

"I know I do nigga."

"You think you tough?" he asked.

"I know I am."

"You can't prove it."

"I know a few people who think so," Bee said.

"And who might that be?"

Bee thought about Blue and Lucky, but they couldn't think anymore. Lil Durk said it best: head shot he won't think again. She decided to lie instead, she didn't wanna run him off when he found out she had more bodies than him.

"My two best friends, and a few bitch's I put hands on," she said, balling her fists up and showing them to him. She looked so cute, he thought.

"And what you gone do with them lil things?" he joked.

"To you nothing, but anybody else can get it."

"Oh, so you got a soft spot for me?"

"I didn't say that," Bee blushed.

"Ya you do, your face is red from blushing."

"No, it ain't. Black people don't blush."

"That's a lie, cause yo ass is right now."

"Boy you crazy."

"What's crazy about me?"

"Nothing, it's a figure of speech. What I really meant to say is you too sexy," Bee said while rubbing his leg. All jokes aside, she'd come for dick, not food. She didn't wanna go on a date, at least not tonight. No! She had other plans, about 9 inches of them.

"Let's just get a room tonight and fuck. We can have a date another time," she added while placing her hand on his lap and grabbing his cock.

"You sure that's what you want?" he asked, as he began to get rock hard.

"Ya I'm sure," she said, opening the fly of his Robin Jeans and leaning her head to his dick, sucking him into her mouth. She kept him on the verge of cumming until they made it to Gammon. She felt they made it too soon, because she didn't wanna stop. They made their way to the room like two love birds unable to keep their hands off each other. As soon as the door closed, Bee pushed him to his knees. She put her foot on a chair and spread her legs lifting her dress up. Her pussy was already soaking wet. Bee grabbed the back of his head rubbing her pussy up and down his face. He loved the way she took charge, and his cock actually hurt. It felt as though it stretched beyond its limits. Bee hardly gave him a chance to open his mouth and stick out his tongue. When he was finally able to put his tongue on her, she moaned and began oscillating her hips while rubbing her clit in a circular motion on the tip of his tongue. She reached down to hold his head as she moaned louder. "Make me cum," she yelled, as she fucked his tongue. He picked up the rhythm of her gyrations. When she rotates one way, he went the opposite making sure to include her clit in his strokes. She moaned and gasped loud while cumming all over his face.

"That was good boi," she said outta breath. "Now it's time for you to fuck my face," she added with a light giggle.

"What's funny?" Martez asked, standing to his feet.

"You don't wanna know."

"Try me."

Bee laughed again, because she'd never been so aggressive with a man before. The way she pushed him to the floor and made him eat her, reminded her of how male porno stars did woman.

"Ok don't get mad," she said, kissing him on the lips. "But I just treated you like a T.H.O.T." He laughed cause it was true.

"You wanna play games?" He asked, picking her up and throwing her on the bed.

"Ya, what you gone do about it?" she asked, licking her lips and spreading her legs, giving him a view of her fat pussy. Martez watched as she took her dress off and showed her body. He undressed himself. "We gone see if you still playing when I'm done with you," he said, getting on top of her. Bee waited impatiently for him to fill her up, but instead of sticking it in, he ran it up and down the outside of her pussy, driving her wild. He sank it partway into her. She was so wired, that she came instantly. He laughed and grabbed her legs and spread them wider, so he could put his thick cock all the way in her. She groaned, god he stretched her! He hadn't even began fucking and she was nearly cumming again. When he started, he fucked her aggressively, bringing her to a wild climax before releasing his load inside her. Bee was so high on sex, she never thought once about what just happened, and neither did he.

"I swear that was the best sex ever," she said after catching her breath.

"Who you telling, this what I do," he joked, and they laughed. She wasn't lying, he'd out done his last performance.

"You too confident! But it adds to the sex appeal," she said kissing him. He held her in his arms while she laid her head on his chest.

"What's your favorite color?" Martez asked out the blue.

"Green, how about you?"

"Black."

"Out of all colors, black?"

"Ya, black is powerful. It's strong, because all it's been through."

"Are you still talking about the color?"

"Not really, but kind of, well I'm talking about the race."

"Please don't say you racist."

"Na ma, it ain't that. It's just, I'm proud to be black because we strong people. I'm not saying other races are weak. I'm just saying we been through a lot as people, that's all."

"Ya, you can say that again."

"So, if you had a wish what would it be?" he asked.

"I don't really know, I guess money! What about you?"

"I would wish our people could come together and get something done as a body."

"Your answer makes mind seem shallow. Here I am thinking of myself, and you're thinking a lot deeper."

"You shouldn't feel shallow, all you asked for is what most people would. There's nothing wrong with that. Now with that said, I believe you're different and should think differently from others, but right now you're young. You gone learn with time that being different is ok."

Bee closed her eyes and thought about everything he said. It was deep, her mind couldn't understand it at this point, but she hoped he'd teach her to understand everything she didn't.

"You sleep ma?"

"Nah just listening to your heartbeat."

"Is it roaring?"

"What?"

"I asked if it is roaring, cause it's the heart of a lion."

"You play too much," she laughed. They laid there getting to know one another before falling asleep in each other arms.

CHAPTER NINE

ee woke up, and Martez was gone. She laid in bed pondering about last night. Damn, she had some proper sex. He was fucking her and in love with him. Her feelings for Martez were too potent too soon.

They'd only had sex twice. She was falling in love with a man she didn't know. Last night they talked and got to know each other a little better, but she still didn't know him entirely, just what he told her. What if he lied about everything, she asked him? He kept her smiling and laughing all night, but what if it was all game. It wouldn't be the first time a man deceived her. But why did he have to lie? What was his reason for running game when they already had sex? He was upfront about not wanting a relationship. Bee laughed at herself, he had no motive to tell fairy tales, she was already giving up the goodies. She was falling for him because he had deeper conversations than most men. The things he said meant something. He'd been straight forward with her about shit most men lied about. Bee experienced anxiety at that moment, she couldn't catch feelings. No! She needed space to breathe and gather her thoughts. She planned to stay away from him, far away. This was becoming a situation she didn't wanna be a part of. She'd seen too many heartbroken women in her lifetime, so she was going to step away before it happened to her. It was time to snap outta whatever emotions she'd been having and get back to business. While she was having the best sex of her life last night, her line was ringing off the hook. She'd miss money for sex. Money, she needed, possibly over 50 bands. The sex was great, but not 50'Gs worth.

She got outta bed in put her clothes back on, once she was dress, she headed home. The instant she got in the cab, Cash Moody's song, "Mr. Wrong" came on.

"She just wanna fuck, cause nigga do too much, and when he ain't around, and you wanna get down, you know to hit me up, and I'm gone beat it down, and we be going hard, I'm her mister wrong, take them clothes off, and we gone get it on, we gone get it on, we can do it in the crib but I prefer to get a room."

Bee asked the driver to switch the song. It was too early for fuck music. The song he switched to wasn't much better, it was Rae Sremmard's "Black Beatles." She thought about asking him to just kill the music and ride in silence but decided not to kill his vibe. He seems to be in a good mood. It wasn't his fault she was having a bad morning. He had no idea she'd fucked a man and woke up alone with a wet pussy and emotional issues she couldn't explain. They pulled up to her house and she paid before going inside. Glory and Black were still sleeping. She woke them up and told them it was time to hit the streets. Glory made the calls to rent the hotels, while Bee waited on Black to finish showering. She sent out the group text, as she always did. *First come first served.* Texts came back in a jiffy. After reading through them, 150 pounds were sold.

This shit crazy, she thought while rubbing her fingers through her hair. She assumed Tez was making this type of money, but now she understood why he lived a lavish life, and wondered if she missed the real jackpot, or if she had gotten all he had. She pushed that thought to the back of her mind, it was too late now. Once Black got out the shower, Bee rushed in and took one herself. It didn't take long to shower and get dress and be out the door. She turned all emotions off the minute she grabbed her pretty savages and hoodie. The only thing on her mind was money, and if something went wrong, she'd catch a body. She got in the car right before Black pulled out. Bee turned on some music. She wanted to be in the right mood just in case she had to pop something.

"Ya they hate that they broke though

And when it's time to pop they a no-show

Ya, I'm pretty but I'm loco

That loud got me moving slow-mo.

Young Ma's "Ooouuu" set the mood. Bee sat back and vibed with the music while gripping her pistols. Black frowned at her sitting there, hoodie on, bobbing her head to the music like a dude.

"Bitch you really think you a killa?"

"If I ain't who is?" Bee smiled.

"You too much."

My brother told me fuck'em get that money, sis

You just keep on grinding on ya hungry shit.

Ignore the hate, ignore the fake, ignore the funny shit.

Cause if a nigga violate, we got a hundred clips.

Bee song along to the music, her pretty savages on her lap.

"Bitch, when I'm getting a gun?" Black questioned. Bee frowned; she didn't like the idea of Black having a gun. Hell no! The bitch was liable to end up shooting herself by mistake.

"As long as I'm alive, you don't need one. If a mathafucka try you, point em out and I'll take care of the rest," Bee stated.

Black shook her head and agreed without hesitation. A part of her wanted a gun, but the other half knew she couldn't take a life. She'd leave the killing to Bee. They pulled up to the hotel and made their way inside. Before they entered the room, they put on gloves. Bee unlocked the room door with her gloved finger. Black set the bag on the bed.

"So, when we gone enjoy some of this money?" Black asked.

"I've been thinking about that," Bee said, sitting on the bed. "Soon, I guess. Why? What you want?" Black thought about it for a moment before saying, "At least a new car, some clothes, and maybe some jewelry. Hell, I'm try'na be iced out like Keyshia Kaior."

"Girl sit yo ass down somewhere," Bee said while laughing.

"What's funny bitch? With the kind of money, we seeing it's possible."

"It is. Girl let's make this flip and then we'll see about getting everything your heart desires."

"You can't help with what my heart desires, it's gone take a big man to do that."

Bee shook her head, and there was a knock on the door. "Get in the bathroom," Black said. Bee didn't move. She wanted to do things differently this time, so the buyer would see the muscle. "Just open the door," Bee said, pulling her pretty savages out.

A Young Thug looking dude walked in behind Black. He was good looking, a lil bit on the short side, and wore all black with black Timberland boots. He had a tough look to him but the moment he saw Bee's savages, he turned pussy.

"What y'all on?" he said, putting his hands in the air. He looked back as the door closed and thoughts of making a run for it flashed in his mind.

"We ain't on shit play boi," Bee said vaguely.

"Look y'all can take this shit," he said, taking the bag off his shoulder and placing it on the floor. Bee smiled before saying, "Now why would we rob you? Come on, we only wanna make sure you ain't gone rob us."

"Hell, nah man, I don't get down like that. I do good business," he said, still worried.

"You could put ya hands down this ain't a stick up." Once he placed his hands on his side, Black handed him the bag. He took the bag before asking Bee, "We cool right?" Bee smiled because he really was asking for permission to leave.

"Nah we ain't." The expression on his face said, ah shit!

"I got something I want to propose to you. Well it's a business opportunity, how about whatever you buy, I front you starting on your next reup?" she said, placing the guns in her pocket. He stared at Bee wondering if this was another test. Once he was sure it wasn't, he smiled. "Hell ya, that sounds good to me. I just got one question, when I gotta pay you? I mean how much time I got?" he asked nervously.

"A month. If you done before that, come back, and we'll do it again. I got a feeling I won't have a problem with you," she said staring at him sideways.

"I do good business, just ask Tez," he repeated.

"Cool, then give me a call when you're ready."

"Cool cool… I can leave now?" he asked.

"Ya," he rushed outta the room. Bee was willing to bet that he thanked god once he was in the hallway. Black looked at her and how much of a thug she was becoming.

"Let's get outta here," Bee said, as if she didn't hold a man at gun point for kicks.

"You loving this shit ain't you?" Black asked, grabbing the bag and opening the door. Bee walked out behind her without responding. Her hands still gripped her tools just in case an ambush was waiting on the other side. They made their way safely to the car and pulled off.

The rest of the day was spent chasing bands, and at the end of the night they had a duffle bag with 375,000 dollars inside. They met people from Chicago and Ohio, but most of them came from all over Wisconsin. Once they made it inside, Bee went to talk to Glory. She was drowsy; it had been a long day. Glory told her that yesterday she talked to a contractor who would do the work. He would fabricate the price and make everything look cheaper than it regularly was. Bee loved how she took responsibility over the legal business. She was being the best businesswoman she could possibly be. She liked how it seemed like she'd prepared for this moment. After talking with Glory, Bee texted Ryan informing him that she needed another shipment. Then, they counted out $300,000 to pay him. Bee received a call from Martez but ignored it. She was try'na focus on money, not a nigga. She really wanted to convince herself that there wasn't any feelings involve. But he stayed on her mind, and the instant she ignored his call, she regretted it. Her mind told her to forget him, but her body was calling his name. In his arms was where she wanted to be, no matter how many lies she told herself. When she closed her eyes, she envisioned his hard dick, and the pleasure it brought, how hard it felt, and the heat. It was amazing. Just the thought of his passion made her abandon her boycott of him. She picked the phone up and sent a text. *I'm horny, can we have another one-night stand?* After sending the text, she felt weak. She'd given into temptation. How come she couldn't get over him like any other man she'd come across? There was no doubt in her mind that the difference was sex. She'd enjoyed it too much. Her phone vibrated. She glanced down and smiled once she saw his response: *"ya, anytime you want."* Bee took another shower and got dressed before telling him what hotel to meet her at. Tonight, would be their final time having intercourse, or at least that's what she hoped. Never having been in love, Bee didn't know her heart belonged to a man. He'd stolen her heart without trying.

(Meanwhile)

A motorcade of black automobiles drove up East Washington. There was a 2018 Lexus RX, XTS Cadillac, Maserati Levante, and a Bentley Bentay Gan.

Cash reclined and the back of the Bentley as his driver drove. He was sipping on a 5th of peach Cîroc and reminiscing about his twin brother, Money, A tear rolled down his face as he thought about someone having his brother's body under their belt. Even though they didn't have the best relationship, he would've died for Money without thinking twice. He loved his brother and wanted revenge for him, if it was the last thing he did.

Team savage was on their way to the studio to meet Slim Cash and his bagz of money gang. They pulled up and found 10 dudes standing out front. Cash watched as his team made sure everything was smooth before he stepped out and went inside. He was killing it in a red Gucci shirt, a pair of white skinny jeans, and red Gucci kicks. His bagz of money chain lit up the night as he stepped in the building. Smoke filled the air and the smell was over the top. Slim Cash walked over, and they shook hands. Team savage spread around him, uneasy being in a room of new faces.

"It's all love in here," Cash said, easing the tensions. That's all it took for them to kick they feet up and take their hands off their pistols. He followed Slim to a room in the back to discuss business.

"What's good skud, how business been?" Cash asked once they were situated.

"Shit going good bro. Moody working hard, and we working on some big features. The studio smoking; it's the best in the town. Almost everybody chasing a rap dream and try'na book time. But it's a waiting list," Slim said and passed Cash a blunt.

"That's what's up skud. I'm looking for some new business partners on the illegal side though. You know any good niggas down here?" Cash asked.

"Ya I know one good nigga, his name K.O. He's been to the feds and never ratted. He did his time like a man. He just coming home from doing 5 years on a pistol case. I could set up a meeting after I see if he still on that." Cash shook his head. "Ya see what he on then get back to me," Cash said, never questioning Slim's judgement, not even once. He'd proven he was trustworthy.

"Bro pass the blunt, you over their baby sitting and shit," Cash joked.

"My bad skud, that loud got me moving slow mo."

"I see nigga!" Cash said, sticking his hand out to shake up after taking the blunt. They heard a lot of laughter come from upfront and went to see what was funny. When they walked in the room, Cash saw Moody was casing with Monty, a good friend of his.

"Boy on Dave, you look like you survived an abortion."

"Boy you look like Eddie Griffin," Monty shot right back.

"Boy you the only nigga that tape a quarter to the side of his leg to say you getting money on the side."

Everyone in the room laughed hysterically. Monty and Moody went back in forth for over an hour as they smoked blunts after blunts. "Aight I'm outta here," Cash said while passing someone the blunt in his hand. He'd reached his limit a while ago but smoked just to be smoking. "Aight skud." Slim stood up and shook hands with him. Team savage exited the building, hands on straps just in case. Cash squatted inside his Bentley before the motorcade pulled off, heading back to Chicago. He came looking for a business partner but ended up having a good time with the Bagz of Money Gang.

*****

Bee was spread out in bed with Martez after another insane session of sex. It was 4:30 AM and she still hadn't been to sleep. After sex, they talked about life and got to know each other. He wanted to know how bad growing up in the system was for her and told her all about his experiences with group homes as a child. Bee told him how hard it was growing up without any parents, which he understood, having gone through most of the same problems. They had a lot in common. When it was time for her to leave, he didn't wanna see her ago. She was really growing on him and his mind was open to the possibility of a relationship. He wanted to spend as much time with her as possible. Bee left at 6am after another round of sex. He got up to take a shower before getting dress. He needed to work on a case this morning. Well really, he never worked on cases himself anymore. His legal team prepared them, and he studied them before trial.

He didn't have a passion for law anymore. It was an occupation he'd chosen for money purposes only. But now that he was thriving and not in need, the study was becoming too much. He wanted freedom to enjoy himself and spend his riches, to have the freedom to take a trip whenever he desired. He put off studying for now, this would be the last case he worked on personally for some time. It was time for a break. He sat around the house and watched ESPN for a while before becoming restless. This wasn't life; he was almost always alone. He began to regret never finding a woman to share all his success with. Maybe Bee was that woman, or maybe he just needed to find something to do, because his mind was wondering into places it had no business with. Love was out of the question or was it because ever since Bee came in his life, his spirit was high. He couldn't remember the last time he'd cared about getting to know a woman inside and out. He loved fucking her, but when he thought about her, that wasn't what came to mind. It was the small things like her smile, her laugh, and just the way she looked at him like he was the most important person in the world. She was special and beyond beautiful, with just the right type of attitude. He couldn't believe he was having thoughts of leaving the player lifestyle behind. It was a life where he didn't have to answer to any woman. He could come and go as he pleased, never having to fight. He was living every man's dream. What if she was the one? What if he missed out on true love? Was the saying, "it's better to love and have lost, then to never have loved at all," actually true? But what if she didn't want a man? What if she didn't have feelings for him? He didn't know. They talked about a lot of things, but not a relationship. She'd been too willing to go along with it. He wondered if she believed in true love. His iPhone vibrated on the nightstand and the screen indicated it was Bee. He smiled before answering.

"Ya what's good?"

"I hope this don't make you uncomfortable, but I miss you," she said.

"Nah, I was thinking about you before you called. You been on my mind all day."

"That's nice to hear."

"So how about we spend the day together?" he asked.

"I want to...believe me, but I gotta run around a few more hours. Then, I'm all yours."

"Cool, just hit me up whenever."

"Nah wait, just give me an hour," Bee said, cutting him off. She'd rush through the rest of the buys. He asked to spend the day with her, and from the sound of his voice, he was a little disappointed. A part of her couldn't let him down, couldn't leave him hanging. She wanted to ride or die, to prove she was a keeper.

"Aight, see you in an hour."

"Ok bye."

He hung up and thought about confessing his true feelings tonight.

(Kia)

After the night of sex, Kia got on top of her business. The sex was great, and she exchanged numbers with Tre Boi afterwards. He made her laugh at the end of the night when he said that he should've been paying her. She told him the money didn't matter before they went their separate ways. Kia planned on hooking up with him again, but right now he was the last thing on her mind, like she was sure she was the last thing on his.

Kia pulled into the parking lot on Allied drive followed by two mini vans of shooters.

One Eye Larry walked outta his building and jumped into the passenger seat.

"Hi Kia," he said, happy to see her for the first time since Money was murdered.

"Hi Larry," she responded before reaching in the back seat and pulling out a kilo of raw boy and handing it to him. Kia expected him to get out, but she looked over and saw him starring at her.

"What?" she asked raising her eyebrow.

"I heard you got married to some African!" he said while placing the work into a bag. "Shit, you forgot about nephew fast," he added, a little upset at her disloyalty. He'd known the twins, Cash and Money, most of their lives and saw them as family. It broke his heart when he heard Money had been murdered in his home. When he got the news, he cried for four nights straight. Money gave him a chance when he needed one. Now, he was off drugs and was pushing weight. His life had changed, and he had them to thank for it. But a part of him felt guilty for being around Kia. He'd heard a few Africans were killed attempting to kill Money. It didn't take much to put two and two together. After his murder, Kia ended up married to an African and now had a caravan of them watching her back. Larry believed she was responsible for having him killed to take over his kingdom.

"No that's not the case Larry, I'll never forget him. I just had to move on," Kia said while putting her head down ashamed.

If Larry was looking to crush her heart he'd succeeded. She felt lower than low hearing those words. It brought out the guilt she'd suppressed the last few months.

"Well I gotta make a run," she added, hoping he got the hint and got out. Larry opened the door and gave her one last disgusted look before closing the door behind him.

A tear escaped her eyes before she wiped it away. *Who the fuck was his hype ass to judge her?*

She helped him stay on his feet and put food in his mouth. *Fuck that hype*, she thought while pulling out of the lot. He'd be lucky if she didn't have him murdered for looking at her the way he did. It was a new day and if he couldn't see the vision, he'd join Money soon.

(An Hour Later)

When they arrived at Outback Steak House, Martez opened her door like a gentleman as always. He got his first back shot of the night in the form of a blue Louis Vuitton bodycon dress. It hugged her body in all the right places. He smacked her backside and she turned around and smirked before saying, "Don't get nothing started we can't finish now." Martez smiled and followed her inside. They took a seat and began looking over the menu.

"So, you didn't get enough of me last night?" she said, grinning from ear to ear. She saw the look in his eyes, he was falling for her. When they started talking, the only thing she saw was lust, but now when he looked at her, she saw fondness, affection, and attachment. All the signs of love on the brain, even if he wasn't ready to admit it yet. When she received his call, she really needed to hear his voice. Her heart melted when he asked to spend the day with her.

"Nah ma, I didn't get enough of you to be honest. You been on my mind all day," he said, sitting back in his seat.

'Ya whatever boy tell that to the next bitch," Bee said playfully.

"I ain't playing ma no lie, you been on a nigga mind since I first met you," he said, placing his hand on hers before continuing. "I know it's kinda fast, but I'm feeling you a lot and I know you might not feel the same but..."

"I do," she said, cutting him off while staring in his eyes. She saw sincerity in them. He was confessing his true feelings. Boy did she hope he wanted her as much as she needed him.

"I wanna stop playing games, and really, really get to know each other."

"I was never playing games, I was giving you what you asked for. But I'm really feeling you as well, and anything you want to know just ask," Bee said, letting her true emotions out for the first time. She felt relieved, like floating on cloud nine. She was high off her emotions for the man who was like a drug to her. She was willing to tell him anything if it meant winning his heart. The feeling she had for him was deeper than she ever imagined possible. She couldn't believe she'd been depriving herself of true love this long. Martez wanted to know if Bee really trusted him. He skipped the bullshit questions and immediately got to the deeper ones.

"How did you get money to open a club?"

Bee was thunderstruck by the question, but something inside told her to trust him. The look in his eyes reassured her that she could. He lived a life similar to hers and had been through some of the same problems. He understood the struggle of the streets, so he should understand her lifestyle.

"I sell Marijuana," she said, giving in. He sat up in his seat with renewed interest. His mind formed questions after questions. How? Why? When? And a few more.

"Stop fucking around, you ain't made that kinda money pushing marijuana, come on ma keep it real."

"No really I did. A friend of mine was killed and he sold loud. When he died, I was able to get his phone and take over the business," she replied reluctantly. A flash of jealousy came over him.

"Was this guy just a friend or a friend with benefits?" he questioned. Bee thought this jealously was cute. Not wanting to begin their relationship with lies, she told him the truth. "We used to mess around," she answered. "Was it serious?" Bee thought about it for a moment. It wasn't serious for her, but Tez loved her. She had love for him but wasn't in love with him.

"Not for me it wasn't."

"What you mean by that?"

"I guess what I'm saying is he was in love with me, but I wasn't in love with him."

"Have you ever been in love?"

"No," she responded.

"Why is that?"

"I guess I never met the right guy."

"Would you know if you did?"

"I think so."

"Tell me something, do I have a chance at your heart?"

"More than a chance."

"What you mean by that?"

"It means, I want to give you not only my heart but all of me," she said. Immediately, she felt a weight lifted off her. Having it out in the open gave her a true chance of having his heart as well.

"You sure about that?"

"More than sure."

"So, what are you going to do to keep yourself safe in the streets?" Martez asked switching subjects.

"I can hold my own weight."

"Oh, is that right?"

"Ya daddy it is," she said, licking her lips. Martez smiled. She was sexy and freaky, and always found a way to turn any conversation into foreplay.

"Ok so what are you doing to wash the money?"

"Wash the money?" she asked confused.

"You have to wash your money through some type of legit business in order to make it clean to spend on shit without going to jail. There's a lot you gotta learn about drug money. You can't just spend it without the feds kicking in your door one day."

Bee thought about the new information she received, and he was correct. She hadn't made any mistakes yet. They hadn't spent any real money. She wanted to learn everything possible about money laundering. Martez noticed her deep in thought. He told her not to worry, any mistakes made, he'd fix for her. "What do you know about money laundering?" she asked.

"I been around the block a few times." He answered her question without really answering it at all. She noticed that he tried dodging the question.

"I didn't ask that, I asked what you know about money laundering," she responded. Martez smiled; she'd busted him on his sidestep of the question.

"I was in the game. Well not was."

"You are right now?" she whispered, astonished with the new revelation.

"Ya but not for long."

"But how? And what."

"It's girl. The how is, I only do it every six months."

"Damn you must be major to do it only twice a year?"

"I do alright," he said, being modest. Bee smiled. She loved a humble man. He didn't have to tell her he was doing well, cause once every six months said it all. With him being a lawyer, he wouldn't risk jail time for pennies.

"Can you show me how to move the right way? So, I'll never get locked up," she asked, turned on by the new revelations about him. It made this professional man look more like a thug. It added to his sex appeal.

"Ya I got ya," he said before they placed their orders. Once the waitress left, they began their conversation where they left off. Bee slid close to him in the booth. He put his arm around her and held her for their first public embrace. She loved the way he smelled and how tight he held her.

"But you're already on the right path. You decided to open a business, which is a good thing. Where the problem lies is where you got the money in the first place. But I'll fix that for you. I'll invest whatever it costs to open your business..." Bee cut him off. "I can't have any investors cause I'm starting this company with my best friends," she said.

"You spoke too soon, you gotta let me finish. It's only an investment on paper, you'll pay me my money back under the table, and within two years, we'll make it look like you bought me out. How does that sound?"

Bee looked at him and he stared back before putting a wet kiss on her lips, which she returned with passion. She broke the kiss but maintained eye contact.

"That sounds wonderful, almost as wonderful as this," she said, rubbing his cock through his pants.

"You something else girl," he said, kissing her again. When their food arrived, they ate and continued to laugh. She learned a lot about being a major player in the drug business, and about him as well. After dinner he invited her to his home.

Martez gave her a tour of his home and afterwards they sat in the living room, sipping Ace of Spades. "You have a really nice place here," she said, laying with her head on his lap while staring up at him and the celling. She was tipsy from the drinks.

"Thank you," he said.

She looked around and couldn't wait to have a place like this. She thought it was crazy that just a few weeks ago she'd been staying in foster care with a lost soul and a cold heart. But now, she had found herself. And maybe even love. Damn! Life changed fast.

"You're too beautiful, I could look at you for a lifetime," he said, running his fingers through her hair.

"Why look when you can touch?" she said, putting his hand on her chest, making her move. It didn't take long before she got what she was looking for and so much more. An hour and four orgasms later, she fell asleep on his chest with a new possibility of love on the horizon.

(The Next Morning)

Bee woke Martez up and said goodbye before leaving. She promised to call when she finished taking care of business. He touched her heart when he said be careful. He seemed genuinely concerned for her safety. Bee took a shower at home and got dressed, then her and Black went to make a dump for 150 pounds. She rode in the backseat as Black drove. Today, they were making the dump outta the car. Martez told her that while doing a drug transaction, she should never let anyone sit behind her because it was easier to blow yo brains out. His advice reminded her of how she got the ups on Lucky and Blue. It made more sense to her than he'd ever know. They pulled up to Walgreens on Whitney Way and parked beside a Chevy Crease. The driver got out and got in the passenger seat. Bee held onto one of her pretty savages as she handed him the duffle bag. He handed her one back. She looked over the cash before giving him the ok to leave. Black pulled out the moment he closed the door. She didn't like this style of business at all. It made her uneasy. What she didn't know was that this was the style used all over Wisconsin. Bee laid across the back seat going through the money. It seemed like it was all there, but she would count it once again at home. "Pull up to the B.P on Allied real quick, I gotta grab something," Bee yelled over the music. Black shook her head and made the left on Raymond Road. They pulled up to B.P., playing Cardi B's, "Lick"

Looking like I caught a lick

Run up on me you get hit

And all my bitches with the shits

Bronx, New York, gansta bitch.

Bee placed her two pistols under the passenger seat before stepping out. There was a lot of people at the gas station with all kinds of whips. Bee looked back at the 2010 Malibu and realized she had to step it up. She believed she had more cash than most niggas, but they were flexing harder than her. She laughed at the niggaz as she opened the store door.

"I wanna know if I can leave a flyer for my club here?" she asked.

"No problem, Bee. I'll give every one of my customers one," the owner said.

"Thank you so much."

"No problem," he said in his heavy accent. Bee grabbed a few things before paying and leaving. She got into the passenger side and pulled her savages from under her. Black turned the music down.

"Do you see these niggas out here flexing?"

"That ain't flexing. Wait until we step out, we gone fuck the city up."

"I can't wait till we done with this club shit," she said while pulling off.

"Me neither, but it won't be too much longer."

They pulled up to the house and Bee took out her phone to call Martez. She wanted to see how his day was going and she wanted to hear his voice. They talked about Glory meeting his people and learning about money laundering. Bee wanted to wash enough money for them new cars. Her friends had no idea she planned on getting them new whips. As their conversation switched, Bee began to smile. It was really starting to feel like they were in a relationship. Her heart dropped out her chest when he asked her to be his woman. She said yes so fast that he laughed at her. But being in a relationship scared her. She really liked him and worried she might get hurt, or worse, run him off. He was older and more mature than her. She prayed she was enough woman for him.

(Meanwhile June)

"What's good skud?" Cash said while stepping out his Mercedes Bens C-Class. June sat on his Land Rover, fresh from head to toe.

"Same shit skud," he answered as they shook up.

"I'm try'na make this quick, but I wanna know if word got around about who killed my brother?" Cash asked, for what seemed like the millionth time. June was sure he knew who killed him, but he didn't have evidence to prove it. And even if he did, he didn't want to tell Cash. The woman that he expected had ordered the hit was possibly his next connect. June's ambition and Cash's poor leadership had them like friends and enemies at the moment. What was once a brotherhood, was now a game of hide and seek for June. He played his part and acted friendly but at times, he was counting down the days of Cash's life. Cash was unaware of his thoughts of betrayal, and always met him with open arms and love. But one day, if Cash hadn't changed for sure, he'd look him in the eyes and blow his brains out. Cash seemed to be changing, but June wanted more proof before calling his plans off.

"Nah ain't no word bro. It's crazy don't nobody know shit… But once we find out I'mma bring them to you."

"I ain't gone lie, that shit killing me. I want the head of the muthafucka responsible. Then I'mma kill their whole family," Cash said coldly. June knew he meant everything he said. Cash didn't have a problem putting out a hit, and June got most of his bodies on Cash's orders.

"But the reason I called you is that I'm bout to step back until I find out who murdered my brother and I want you to look over things for me," Cash said. He trusted June over everyone on his team and believed that this was the right decision. June didn't know what to say. A part of him was honored Cash put him in charge. But the other part, saw the opportunity to meet his clientele, and keep them if he had Cash killed.

"Me skud? You know I'm new to this hustling shit. This might be too much responsibility to soon."

"Nah, you a born king, and one day you'll be the crowned king. I know you'll do a good job. I trust you Skud," Cash said, sticking his hand out and shook up. He stared in June's eyes for any sign of disloyalty but saw none. June had the poker face of a professional.

"Don't worry bro, find out who killed yo people, and I'll hold it down."

"Love skud. I'mma call you when it's time to introduce you to the clientele."

"Love skud," June said as Cash got in his vehicle. A smile spread across his face as Cash pulled off. Cash might've just made the biggest mistake of his life and didn't even know it. June planned to hit a few more licks and continue to run his team as he waited to hear from Kia. Then, it might be lights out for anyone standing in the way.

CHAPTER TEN

Two weeks Later

Bee sat in the movies watching "Get out" with Martez. Over the last two weeks, she'd slept at his house every night. They spent most of their time together, and she was sure she loved him. There was nothing as amazing as being with him. He treated her with respect, fucked her good, and seemed to love her back. They hadn't shared those 3 words with each other yet, but it went without saying. They both felt the love, and words wouldn't make it any more authentic. They didn't need to say it, because what's understood doesn't need to be explained. She glanced over at him and saw her future husband and smiled. She was so happy at this point in her life, she couldn't help but laugh and smile all the time. She was making an abundance of money and had someone who cherished the ground she walked on. What more could she ask for? She stared at her man who seemed to be enjoying the movie that she could care less about, so her mischievous side kick in. She scanned the movie theater. They were seated alone in the back, so she felt safe enough to drop to her knees in front of him. Martez was startled for a second, but quickly gave into pleasure, as she freed his cock. She smiled up at him before taking him in her mouth. She stroked him as she sucked for a minute. Bee stick her tongue out and licked the precum from his slit. She began swirling her tongue around his cockhead and all over it. She went around the sides and across the top, and then she began licking up and down the full length of his shaft. Bee sucked him and gently squeezed and massaged his fully loaded balls. She was enjoying herself as Martez laid back with his eyes closed. Finally, after teasing him with her wet tongue until he started to squirm, she opened her mouth again as wide as she could and slowly slid down his length. She started to suck him, first moving her wet mouth slowly up and down his thick dick, then quickly picking up speed. She was bobbing her head rapidly, taking more and more of him into her mouth with each downward stroke, until she buried her nose into his pubic hairs. This set him off. He grunted and his whole body shivered; he had filled her hot mouth with nut. He shot 3 forceful blasts of nut into her mouth. Bee let out a soft moan as she made slurping sounds. Only once his cock was completely limp did she release it from her lips and sat up and sighed. Martez put his limp tool back into his pants, unable to speak.

"I'm mad you ain't have enough cum for me daddy," Bee said a little upset.

"Girl, you been sucking and fucking the shit outta me for the last two weeks," he said, kissing the side of her face. Bee eased up on the little attitude, because he was right. Every time his dick got hard it was cause she wanted to fuck. She didn't know why she'd been so horny lately, but he gave her all the sex she wanted.

"Well I ain't give you none for a week. Next time it'll be more than a mouth full," she said. He laughed. She was a boss freak.

"Come on ma, let's go home."

"But the movie ain't over."

"You knew I wouldn't be able to watch the rest of the movie when you pulled that shit because I hate missing the smallest part of a movie."

Bee laughed; she was busted. "It wasn't good anyways," she said, standing up and walking down the stairs. Martez looked at her ass and felt lucky to call her his woman. She had everything a man wanted. Bee was intelligent, beautiful, and had sex appeal. She catered to his every need. If he wanted a massage after a long day of work, she asked how long. If he spent days studying for a case, she'd stayed as quiet as possible, allowing him to work. She was independent, and never asked him for anything. So, he never thought she was using him for his wealth. He followed her out the theater. Once they were outside, he hugged her from behind and placed kisses all over her neck. They walked to the car while embracing each other.

"You make me feel like the luckiest woman in the world," she said, turning to face him. They stared in each other eyes. She could spend the rest of her life in this moment. As long as he held her down, she didn't plan to leave.

"I feel like the lucky one," he said, holding her tight.

"I guess we're both lucky... I think I'm in love with you," Bee said.

"You think?"

"No, I know I'm in love with you."

"I love you to girl," he responded.

Her heart melted after hearing those words for the first time.

"Come on daddy, I changed my mind. I need to be fucked good and hard tonight." Martez opened the door, more than willing to give her what she wanted.

(Meanwhile)

Reese sat in his cell at Waupun Correctional Institution. His mind was on the release date Martez got him a few weeks ago. He was glad to be coming home after years behind bars. He did pushups in segregation. His whole bid was spent in and out of seg. He fought more times than he cared to count. He stood up out of breath and looked over his freedom papers. Three months left, then he'd be inside some pussy. He'd be able to come and go as he pleased. Thoughts of all the money Martez had waiting on him made him do another set of pushups to contain his excitement. After another set of 50, he stood up and threw a few punches at the air. "Just 3 more months until I'm a free man," he yelled so the whole prison heard him.

(2 Hours Later)

Bee walked down to the kitchen for some water after amazing sex. The whole time while they were making love, she told him over and over how she loved him. She grabbed two bottles of water before heading back upstairs. Martez was sleeping, so she put a bottle on the nightstand next to him. Before getting in bed, Bee picked up her phone and called Glory.

"Hello!" Glory said sleepily.

"You asleep?"

"Bitch not no more."

"Good cause I need to talk."

"About what? Because I would love to go back to sleep."

"Martez told me he loved me," Bee said, smiling from ear to ear.

"That's good tell me about it in the morning."

"Bitch I'm sharing a moment with you."

"Share it with Black, then I'll act like this conversation never took place, and I'll be surprised to hear it tomorrow. You won't even know I'm faking."

"Come on Glory get up," Bee pleaded.

"Ok, I'm up, so what you say once he told you he loved you?"

"Well I said it first."

"Stop playing. Not yo tough ass."

"It's not like that with us. I let myself go around him. I can really be me without him judging me.

"That must be nice... I've never had that before with a boy."

"Martez is a man, not a boy. He got 9inchs to back that up."

"Didn't need to know that."

"Oh, my bad, but I'm really in love with him. It's crazy and scary at the same time. I've never been in love before. What if I'm not enough woman for him?"

Martz rolled over and kissed her neck. Before saying, "You're more than enough." Bee turned and kissed him before the phone fell from her ear as they kissed passionately. Glory heard a loud moan before hanging up.

CHAPTER ELEVEN

3 Months Later

*B*ee rolled up to opening night at Deception Night Club in her 2018 Audi AS Coup, and behind her was a 2018Audi A3 and a Audi A6. Over 3 months had passed and life for them had changed in so many ways. Ryan was fronting her 500 pounds a month with an unlimited supply of molly, Xanax, and syrup. The street was calling her the queen of the trap. Things with her and Martez were going wonderfully. She'd moved out and into his mansion. Glory and Black had their own places in downtown at the Madison High Rise apartments. Bee was head over hills in love. In Martez, she found everything a woman could dream of and so much more.

The valet opened her door and she stepped out. All eyes were on the queen of the trap. It reminded her of the tabloid waiting to see Kim Kardashian. Everyone wanted to know what she was wearing, and she didn't disappoint with her pink and white Gucci dress and Jimmy Choo. Bee felt like a star, and tonight she was. They made their way inside by passing the line of onlookers and even a few hating hoes into their club.

The party was in full swing. The DJ was doing his thing and shouting them out as they made their way to the V.I.P. section. When the waitresses spotted them, they began to cater to their bosses. Champagne began flowing their way.

Cardi B's hit song "Bodak Yellow" came on and the club went crazy. Bee began to dance along with Glory and Black.

Said little bitch, you can't fuck with me If you wanted to These expensive, these is red bottoms These is bloody shoes, Hit the store, I can get 'em both I don't wanna choose And I'm quick, cut a nigga off So don't get comfortable Look, I don't dance now I make money moves.

Bee loved the part about red bottoms, and she liked it even more tonight since she was wearing them

"I can't believe we own this place," Glory yelled over the music, so they could hear her.

"Me either," Black said, looking around amazed at how many people showed up.

"You bitches better believe it then," Bee yelled hugging them. Before taking a seat at their table, she looked up and saw Martez and his friends walking in surrounded by 40 niggas. Bee's heart warmed from peeking at the love of her life. Everyone with him was dressed in trap clothing, but he wore a Tom Ford suit, looking professional as always. He made his way over to them. "How y'all doing?" he asked, speaking to everyone before kissing her on the lips. "I want y'all to meet my boys Cash and Reese," he said introducing them. This my girl Bee, this Black, and this Glory," he added. Black noticed how fine Cash was, but he wasn't paying her any attention. His focus was on finding the real party he'd heard about. Cash waved at everyone, just going through the motions.

"It's nice meeting y'all and all, but I'm try'na get to the black card party, A.S.A.P.," he said while rubbing his hands together.

Martez smiled. Cash didn't do anything halfway. If it wasn't the best, he didn't want it.

"Everyone good with you?" Bee questioned, asking if any snitches were with him, because the black card party was over the top and highly illegal. Cash screwed his face up, looking at Bee like she was crazy. "Ask yo man about my team, ain't no rat's in sight fuck…" Before he could continue, Martez cut him off. "They good ma," he said, giving her a kiss on the lips. Bee frowned at Cash for a moment cause he was about to say something disrespectful. He glared back letting her know he wasn't the nigga to play with. Bee wished she had her savages with her at the moment, because she'd body him without losing sleep. She stood up and told them to follow her. They went up a flight of stairs before passing 3 armed bodyguards. They entered the black card party and the room was filled with smoke and naked woman. All the big-time hustlers were partying and watching the ladies strip. They had a codeine bar, where you could find molly, Xanax, and different kinds of loud. There was also a small dispensary back there.

"Now this is what the fuck I'm talking about," Cash yelled over the music. Already knowing the drill, one of his hitters handed him a Louis V bag full of hundreds.

"Let's turn this bitch upside down," Cash yelled and threw a hand full of hundreds in the air. Once the stripper saw he wasn't throwing ones, it was a stampede as they fought for his attention. Black smiled. He was her type… sexy and flamboyant. It didn't take long for Cash's team to break off and turn up, leaving Bee alone with her man.

"How you feeling tonight ma?"

"Good daddy," she said, kissing him on the lips.

"This place turned out nice," he said, admiring the club.

"I know, Glory did a good job."

"No bullshit," Martez said, before laughing and pointing at Cash and Reese. They were all up in Glory's face, but she didn't look interested. Bee laughed because Glory hated thugs. They didn't stand a chance with her. It didn't matter how much money they had. She liked what she liked, and they weren't it.

Martez walked up behind Bee and kissed her on the neck.

"I love you ma," he whispered in her ear.

"I love you more baby."

"I ain't coming home to night. I'm going to California with Reese to party for a few days," he said, putting his tongue in her ear. Bee let out a low moan and was turned on. She thought about him going on a trip for days to party. She was cool with it because she trusted him with all her heart.

"OK daddy, that's too bad because I wanted some tonight."

"When don't you want none?" he joked and laughed.

"Imma go party with my bros, then I'll catch you before I leave," he said kissing her once more.

"OK boo," she said as he walked off. There was so much smoke in the air it was crazy. *Cash was really showing his ass,* Bee thought to herself.

But what she didn't know was that this was his element. He felt at home in the limelight and made sure they knew he was the king.

She liked his swag, and he was a little cute. But if he ever disrespects her, she'd take his life.

*****

Black's pussy was moist from watching Cash. There was nothing sexier than a powerful thug. The instant she saw him, her mind was set. She was going home with him.

She thought Glory was gone give her some competition when she saw them talking but remembered she didn't like thugs.

Black made her move by sending a waitress to him with a bottle of Ace of Spades along with her number and a note that said, *I'm it for the night.*

The waitress pointed her out as she gave him the bottle.

Cash looked over and waved as he put the number in his phone.

"What you doing over here alone?" Bee asked while taking a seat next to her at the bar.

Black smiled at her sister and best friend. Bee was tipsy and enjoying herself. The music was playing, and the mood was right. She was in her vibe.

"Girl you don't wanna know," Black said, rolling her eyes and sipping from her drink.

"Bitch don't tell me what I wanna know. Cause that makes me wanna know even more. As much as you in my business I shouldn't have to ask..."

Black laughed. Bee was right, she stayed in her tea.

"OK since you being noisy, I'm try'na get some dick."

"From who?" Bee shot back, raising an eyebrow.

"Cash."

"Girl that's a grow man, yo little ass fast as hell...I really don't like him," Bee frowned. "But if you gone go for it don't let him know you underage," she added. Even though she didn't like Cash, she supported her girl getting some. It's been close to a year since Black had sex.

It was about time, Bee thought.

"Why you don't like him??? Because he turn me the fuck on," Black said while twisting around in her seat.

"First off bitch slow the fuck down, you acting like you gone cum just thinking about the dick," Bee joked and they laughed. "But for real though it doesn't matter why I don't like him. The only thing that matter is you putting it on him," she added.

"Putting it up on who? Who gone be putting it on somebody?" Martez questioned, walking up on the conversation.

"Nothing boy," Black said, then playfully punched him in the arm.

"I'm finna get outta here baby," he told Bee while she rubbed his arm.

"Wait I gotta talk to you about something important before you leave. It's only gone take a second," Bee said, taking his hand leading him to her office. Black laughed cause Bee didn't have shit to talk about.

At that moment she received a text, from an unknown number:

Meet me at the door in 5 minutes.

*****

"What's so important, "Martez asked when they entered her office.

Bee walked over to her desk and sat down.

"Come here daddy. You know why I called you up here," Bee said, picking up a letter opener. She leaned back in her seat and slowly pulled up her skirt past her thighs, revealing a pink thong that tightly cupped her pussy.

She slid the letter opener down her flat stomach and under the top of her thong as Martez looked on speechless.

She cut her thong off and tossed it away.

She spread and opened her pink pussy lips.

Martez watched, loving the show.

"Come suck my clit daddy."

He got on his knees instantly, putting his mouth on her. He sucked and licked with a hunger which had her cumming in seconds.

"I need to be fucked," she yelled. He looked at her and thought it wouldn't hurt Reese to wait just a little longer.

(1 Hour Later)

Black laid naked in bed with Cash between her legs. She wasn't disappointed. His dick was huge, much bigger than anyone form her past.

She couldn't wait for him to fill her up. He thrust into her and she moaned with pleasure and pain. Only the head was in and she felt full.

It took another ten minutes to work the rest into her. Once he hit the bottom, she thought about how full she felt, as he rolled his hips. Black was seconds away from the best orgasm of her young life. When it hit, it was nothing short of amazing.

When they finished, he rolled off her and breathed heavily.

"Damn ma you got the best pussy I ever had...Shit I'mma have to keep yo ass around."

Black didn't respond, she was lost for words. All she thought about was him finding out her age. Cash sat up in bed and took a sip of his lean.

"Here ma try this," he said passing the cup.

She took a sip, then another one, and fell in love with the taste. Cash rolled up a blunt as Black downed the rest of the drink.

"That shit good ain't it?"

"Ya!" Black said, putting her head in his lap try'na revive his cock.

(The Next Morning)

Martez and Reese arrived in California early in the morning and got picked up by a limousine. They were dropped off at Post Ranch Inn.

The sun shined as beautiful women seemed to be everywhere, they looked. He wanted to introduce Reese to the life of a millionaire. Once they arrived at the hotel, Reese ordered 5 high class escorts for himself.

He'd waited years to get some pussy, and for him, this trip was a nonstop party. He was about to make up for lost time and fuck every bitch possible.

When he got locked up, they didn't have nothing. Now everyone around him was rich.

He was living the life a nigga in prison only dreamed of coming home to. What he didn't know was that Martez worried he'd let the money change him like so many others.

While Reese was down the hall getting his party on, Martez laid back in bed watching ESPN.

He picked up his phone and called Bee.

"Hi baby," she answered, excited to hear from him.

"Hi ma, what you doing?"

"Nothing right now, waiting for tonight to meet this new customer," she responded.

"Be safe...." he said, his voice filled with worry. "I wanna talk to you about something when I get home," he added.

"Everything cool?" she questioned.

"Ya we gotta talk about life."

"Why we can't talk right now?" she said, unwilling to wait.

"I guess that's fine," he said reluctantly before continuing.

"I really ain't feeling this hustling thing no more. I don't like you out there playing with yo life for a few dollars. I got enough money to take care of us. I want you outta the game."

There was a pause on the line. Bee thought about a response. She wasn't ready to leave the game.

She loved Martez and believed he'd take good care of her. But she wanted independence. He was rich, not her. She didn't like the idea of being dependent on a man. Now that she was independent, she wasn't try'na go back to the past.

They made their own money now. Even though it was split three ways, it was still theirs.

She'd saved up $300,000, but it wasn't enough to last the rest of her life.

"You still their ma?"

"Ya baby, I'm here.... How about we talk about this when you get home," she said, unable to come up with excuse at the moment.

He heard the hesitation in here voice, so he didn't force it. He'd try convincing her later. But he'd be lying if he said he wasn't hurt that she didn't trust him enough to believe he'd take care of her.

"Cool see you in two days," he said, disappointed.

"OK daddy love you," Bee said, hearing the disappointment in his voice.

"A'ight," he said, before hanging up in her face. He threw the phone on the bed and headed to join Reese and the escorts.

Reese opened the door, and all he wore was boxers. Martez saw the 5 naked white women on the bed.

"What's good skud?" Reese asked, smiling.

"Try'na party these bitches with you. That's what's up," he said, stepping in the room to cheat for the for first time.

(Later That Night)

"Where the fuck is Black?" Bee yelled, entering Glory's apartment. Glory walked out of her room in boy shorts.

"Why the fuck you yelling?" she asked, confused.

"Have you seen Black? I've been calling this bitch all day and she ain't answering her phone. I even went to her crib. I hope she ok! But if she is, imma kill this bitch for making me miss this move with this new customer," Bee said, worried and pissed at the same time.

This wasn't like Black, not even a lil bit. "Have you seen her since she went with that dude, Cash?" Bee questioned as Glory looked lost in thought.

"Nah, try calling again," she suggested. Bee dialed the number again but got the voice mail.

"Imma kill this bitch," she whispered.

Glory went in her room to get dressed, knowing how much this hustling thing meant to Bee. If Black was alright, they'd be fighting over the missed opportunity. Ever since they started hustling, Bee changed a lot. The power and the money seemed to consume her.

Glory thought they made enough money a long time ago. She wanted to stop this when they opened the club. But Black and Bee wasn't hearing it.

She stepped outta her room ready to go. Black owed her one, Glory thought, knowing she was somewhere laid up with Cash.

"Ok let's go," she said dress in all black, a trapper's uniform. Bee smiled at Miss dependable, who was always ready to step up.

"Let's go," Bee said.

(Meanwhile)

Black was out for the count from good dick and purple syrup.

She'd been sipping and fucking for the last two days. The taste of the drink fooled her into drinking 4oz alone. Her body couldn't bear so much, and it gave in to drowsiness.

She was in a coma-like state, and her phone ringing off the hook until it died. Cash stepped outta bed and looked at her naked body.

Her locks hung to the middle of her back. His dick hardened but ached from all the sex they'd had.

He couldn't get enough of her. He picked up his phone and saw the missed calls before putting it down.

The only person's calls he'd return was June's. He got back in bed and rubbed Black's ass, hoping for another round of great sex, but she was out.

*****

Glory and Bee sat at a table inside the club discussing business with June. Bee's phone vibrated, and she stared down at it. The call was from Martez. Glory seemed to have things under control, so she stepped away to take the call upstairs in her office. Glory played her new role as a trap star well. On the way over, Bee informed her of everything she needed to know for the deal to be a success, and she'd done a great job so far.

Once upstairs, Bee sat in her office talking with her pretty savages in hand, just in case things went south.

"So, do we have a deal or not?" Glory asked.

"You too pretty to be doing this ma," June said. He saw how young she was, about his age. She was stunning, so he meant his words. Her looks couldn't save her.

"Ya we got a deal," he continued.

"We can't have a deal if I don't see no fucking money," Glory said, a little uneasy. There was something about him that made her jittery.

His face was innocent, but his eyes were deadly. She was outta her element, and face to face with a savage. Her gut told her so.

June picked up his phone and called, his girl Kim.

"Bring the money in baby," he said into the receiver.

Glory's eyes widened at the idea of someone else entering the building.

"We never said anything about somebody else attending this meeting," she said, feeling her heartbeat rising.

"I know you ain't think I was gone take the chance of being robed...What the fuck this look like shorty?" he said staring in her eyes.

As they had a stare off, the doorman waited for Glory's approval to let the woman enter, who sat at the door with the bag in hand.

"Let her in Rob," Glory said. He opened the door and patted her down before letting her enter. "She clean boss," he yelled to Glory.

Kim walked over and sat the money on the table, as the bodyguard locked the door behind her. He left them alone a moment and went to grab the pounds of weed from the back room.

Glory skimmed over the money, she estimated it was all there.

"Everything's good," she told the bodyguard. He handed June the bag. The split second he took his eyes off Kim, she pulled a .22 pistol from under her dress.

Boc!

The shot to the side of the head made parts of this brain spatter against the wall in onto Glory's face.

He collapsed to the floor and his body convulsed until it slowly came to rest. Glory froze. She couldn't move, couldn't wipe the blood from her face. She couldn't believe what she'd just seen. June was up in a flash taking the .9mm off the guard's dead body. Everything was moving in slow motion for Glory as the woman held her at gun point, while grabbing the money off the table.

Kim was unable to pull the trigger on the baby-faced teenager. While she hesitated, Bee stepped outta her office, guns in the air.

She aimed at Kim and fired, but June pulled her outta the way before the wave of bullets rained down on her. Instead of hitting their target, they sprayed the wall where she'd just been.

June pulled Kim to the exit while launching 3 rounds at Glory.

Boc! Boc! Boc!

The bullets found a place to rest in her face and upper chest, knocking her outta her chair.

At the sight of Glory's body sprawled on the floor, Bee continued to discharge her firearm until they made it outta the club. She wanted to give chase but couldn't leave Glory laying there.

She bent down. Glory held her throat desperately trying to breath but couldn't. Bee looked at it, a bullet went through her throat. Trying to breathe was useless.

"Breathe, Glory, breathe," Bee said softly as she took out her phone and called for help. She watched Glory take her last breath before she could dial the number. Tears poured down her face as she held her sister.

She stared into her lifeless eyes, and thoughts of the dreams she had that would never be consummated. They would never share a moment with each other again. She knew she'd never be the same after seeing the frightened look in Glory's eyes as she passed away.

The streets were cold hearted, and it was a shame she had to lose someone so dear to feel how freezing cold they could be.

She sat there holding Glory for 20-minutes while wishing god would give them a do over.

CHAPTER TWELVE

Two Weeks Later

fter the shooting, Bee called Martez back for help. She didn't know what to do. He sent a cleanup crew to remove the bodies and any signs that a shooting took place.

Glory's body was found in North Port Apartments, where there was camera footage of 3 masked men dumping her there. Bee was sickened with guilt for letting them dispose of her in such a manner. But she didn't have a choice, or at least she felt she didn't. A few days later, their stepfather ID the body. He called Bee to inform her that he wasn't paying for the funeral of a runaway.

So, Bee took care of the funeral arrangements. Today was the day of the funeral, and Black hadn't talked to Bee since before Glory was murdered. She'd been trying to call but got no answer. Bee spent 95% of the last two weeks in bed. The pain she felt was deeper than the ocean.

Glory didn't deserve this. She had a good heart and was such a good person. The look in her eyes during her last moments was the only thing Bee saw at night. Over and over she had the same nightmare.

She couldn't sleep and Martez was worried about her. It felt like weeks since he last saw her eat.

He was sympathetic to her pain and did everything to accommodate her needs. He wanted her to feel safe, but he couldn't understand her pain until he lost someone he loved. Until then, he'd never comprehend the pain she felt inside. He'd never know the guilt she felt for not protecting her sister. The pain would last a lifetime.

"Bee, come on ma it's time to get up," Martez entered the room and said. Once she didn't move, he went and sat down next to her on the bed. Bee laid there with her face in the pillow.

"I'm not going," she yelled in the pillow before rolling over to turn her back to him.

"Come on ma, you gotta go or you'll never forgive yo self," he said, rubbing her back.

He was right, she couldn't disrespect Glory's memory by not attending her funeral. She got up without saying a word and went to take a shower. Ever since Glory's death, she withdrew from him.

Once she was in the shower, tears ran down her face and mixed in with the water. Bee thought about getting away after the funeral, she needed a little time alone.

She had used her savings to pay Ryan for the pounds she lost, then used Glory's savings to reup when the time came. She planned to think about whether she wanted to continue this lifestyle.

*****

Black's heart was all over the place. One part of her was happy with the last two weeks of her life. She'd been with Cash ever since they met, he wouldn't let her leave his side.

He rented her a high-rise apartment in downtown Chicago after her and Bee got into it to keep her close. Black thought he was in love with her because anything she wanted, she got without question. She had every reason in the world to be happy, but she was hurting worse than ever. The guilt for her part in losing her friend was tearing her apart. Bee wouldn't answer her calls at a time when they needed each other the most.

She felt alone for the first time in years. Why did she sip that lean? If she hadn't, Glory would still be alive. She'd still have her sisters to depend on.

Tears soaked her face as she drove up the interstate to go pay her respect. The music had her in her feelings and took her back to a better time. Cash leaned over and kissed her tears.

"It gone be OK," he said.

She smiled at him. He'd been amazing and held her down at a time when Bee left her to the wolves.

(Beloit Wisconsin)

The buzz of a tattoo gun could be heard as June and Kim got 6-point stars tattoos. He got his on his chest and Kim got 3 behind her ear. June was bossing up every day that passed. His heart was made of ice. The only people he loved was his team back in Chicago, his mom, his dead brother, and his ride or die, Kim.

When it came down to protecting them anybody could get it. He caught his first body at 16 and has been laying shit down since.

Everything he knew about the street came from Cash. When he was young, he admired him more than anyone in the world. He didn't like how Cash spoon fed them and never let them get ahead or do their own thing.

June got his opportunity to come up when Cash sent him to murder a nigga in Beloit. After the kill, he saw the city open for the taking. It didn't take long for him to put his mark on the city and kill the major players.

His mind flashbacked to the murder he commuted two weeks ago. It was the first time he regretted pulling the trigger. He never expected them to be so young. When his man told him about the lick, he said they robbed him at a hotel. He never said they were teenagers. The plan was to kill everyone at the meeting, but the bitch that came down the stairs was prepared for war.

Even though he regretted it, it had to happen. He didn't care if he was fingered for murder, but it would've killed him for Kim to do a life bid. He wasn't leaving any witness, young or old. She had to go and so did her pistol totting friend, there was no questions about that.

Kim passed him a blunt and he took a pull. She stared into his eyes. She knew what he was thinking, it was all she'd thought about. The murder of the girl weighed heavy on her heart, and June knew it. He made his mind up; he wouldn't take her on anymore licks. She meant too much to lose in battle. The next lick he'd take Kutta or Bullet Row.

(Madison)

The funeral had already begun when Black pulled up with Cash and his entourage. Her heart pounded in her chest with fear of what Bee would do once she saw her. Cash sensed her fear and placed his hand on her thigh.

"I ain't gone let nothing happen to you, on Dave," he said, looking into her eyes. Black glanced at the man she was falling in love with and got the strength to go pay her respects.

The moment they entered the ceremony, all eyes were on them. Bee glanced at her and she saw the pain in her eyes as tears ran down her face. She wanted to run to her and beg for forgiveness, but she rolled her eyes and turned around. Their friendship was no more, and it cut her deep. They took a seat, and over the next hour, the pastor gave one of the best speeches she had ever heard. Being inside the church reminded her of her parents passing... the suffering, the crying, and being miserable. At that moment, she felt it all over again.

Anyone attending who knew Glory personally was in tears.

When the funeral was over, Black tried making a quick exit. She didn't go view the body. She couldn't stand seeing her like that. She wanted to remember her as the beautiful person she was.

When she made it to the parking lot her neck snapped back as Bee pulled her hair from behind, yanking her to the ground.

"Go look at her bitch and see what you did," Bee yelled, and Black felt a sharp pain in her left eye, as Bee landed a hard blow. Bee wanted Black to see how her carelessness cost their sister her life. She wanted her to look at Glory's once beautiful face, now altered buy a bullet wound.

Cash pushed Bee forcefully to the ground before she could stick her again. Martez grabbed Cash around the neck.

Team Savage pulled their firearms out and pointed them at him. Once he saw all the pistols pointed in his direction, he released Cash and helped Bee off the ground. She was enraged and shoved him off her, sprinting to her car.

They all watched as she pulled two guns from under the driver seat. Martez held her back. He didn't wanna see anything happen to her, they were outnumbered and out gunned.

"Damn Cash that bitch wanna get down on you," one of his hitters joked.

"She ain't a bitch," Black said while holding her eye and still defending her old friend even after the attack.

Cash looked at her like she was insane.

"Let's just go," Black added, not wanting anyone to get hurt. They thought Bee was a joke. They didn't know she'd kill one of them, but Black knew she would. She respected her anger as a possible blood bath waiting to happen.

Cash saw the fear in Black's eyes, and it pissed him off. Any woman of his would have to have heart to stand up for herself. She would have to be heartless to everyone but him.

"Imma let it go this time, because I know that's yo girl. But if you ever let another bitch put, they hands on you, we ain't got shit else to talk about," he said, before walking to his car. Black followed him wondering how Bee could snake her after all they'd been through.

(Meanwhile)

"Get yo fucking hands off me," Bee yelled at Martez, pissed she had to watch Black and Cash get away. She was gone murder Cash for putting his hands on her.

"Nah ma, I ain't gone let you do this in front of all these people," he said, wiping the tears from her eyes.

"I know you hurting, but this ain't the time or the place," he continued.

She broke down in his arms. He held her as she cried. "I can't believe she gone," she cried.

"I know ma, I know...but you gotta get it together," he said, taking the guns slowly outta her hands and helping her in the car, as tears continued to fall. His heart broke just watching the woman he loved suffering. He wished there was something he could do to take the pain away. But only time would heal her. He closed her door and walked around to the driver side and hopped in. Bee's head was laid against the window as she balled her eyes out. Martez placed his hand on her back to show his support.

"You gotta pull through baby. It's gone be-"

"Don't you fucking tell me it gone be alright," Bee turned around yelling.

"You weren't there, you didn't look yo best friend in the eyes as she took her last breath," she added with hate in her voice.

Martez looked at her and tried being sympathetic to what she was going through. She turned away and stared out the window. He tried finding the words to comfort her, but found none, so he pulled off and headed home.

They arrived at their house 20 minutes later. Bee got out and went inside. Martez pulled out the lot and called Reese.

"What's good skud?" Reese answered.

" I need to link up with ya real quick," Martez said, getting right to the point.

"What's wrong B," Reese asked, able to hear it in his voice.

"Man, it's the nigga Cash...He put his hands on my woman."

"Stop it, bro ain't do no shit like that! Wait fuck that, what you do when he hit her?" Reese added before he could respond.

"Bro I couldn't do shit...He had them young niggaz up on me."

"Ya come get me bro outta pocket. I'm gone call him and have him link with us ASAP," Reese said before hanging up.

Martez threw the phone one the passenger seat. He was ready to put hands on Cash for the years of low-key disrespect. He was done playing games with him. Even though they grew up together, they were never good friends. But ever since he got plugged, Cash was hating on him, and his hatred intensified over the years.

He knew their problem steamed from Cash having to go through him for product. Cash always wanted to be the boss, and never wanted to be under anyone.

When Martez pulled up outside, Reese came out with a small duffle bag and jumped in. He pulled a mac-11 from the bag and placed it on his lap.

"What's that for?" Martez stared at the firearm before pulling off.

"It's for them young niggaz, just in case they wanna show they ass," he said, gripping the Mac in his hands.

Martez laughed, glad to have his best friend home, cause he was an animal when it came to pistol play. He'd murder a nigga without thinking twice. When they pulled up on allied, Cash and his clan of savages were waiting their arrival. They parked in one of the lots before stepping out. As they walked over to Cash and his team, Reese had the mac-11 on a shoestring around his neck. It was behind his back to conceal it.

Cash stood there smiling. "I see you had to run to big bro, like the bitch nigga you-"

Martez hit Cash with a left hook that cut him off and put him on his ass at the same time. His team went for their pistols, but Reese pulled his machine gun before they could reach theirs. "Everybody on the ground," he shouted. They all were quick to drop except two. "Cash let these niggas know I don't repeat myself."

Cash looked at Reese and was upset that he was once again choosing Martez's side. He gave his niggaz the ok to get down, not wanting to lose anyone. They slowly dropped to the ground. Cash stood to his feet and looked at Martez smiling.

"That's what we on Reese?" he asked, wiping the blood from the corner of his mouth.

"Nah, it ain't even like that. You know how we get down, but these niggaz don't. When we got problems, we get it up and leave that shit alone. Y'all know how it goes, so do y'all thing," he said without taking his eyes off Cash's team. He'd heard the stories about team savage while in the pin. So, he wasn't taking them lightly. If he slipped up, they wouldn't hesitate to kill him.

Martez glanced away and Cash hammered him with two blows, knocking him backwards. He threw up his hands and got into a fighting stance.

"I'm finna beat yo ass," Cash said, advancing on him. Martez threw a jab that landed on Cash's nose, causing blood to spill. But it didn't stop him from coming forward. Cash rushed him, picked him up off his feet, and slammed him to the pavement. Dust flew up as their bodies hit the ground. Cash tried getting on top of him, but Martez was too strong to hold down.

They stood up and threw their hands back up. Cash advanced on him once again, moving his head side to side like Mike Tyson. Martez backed up, try'na use his reach advantage, but Cash wasn't having it. He got close enough to throw and landed 5 punches that slammed into his face. He was too fast for Martez, so he grabbed him and slammed him before getting on top of him. Martez was able to land a few blows before Reese said, "that's enough."

He got off Cash and saw the look in his niggaz's eyes as they laid on the ground. They weren't used to being on the other side of the gun. They were hunters, not prey, and Reese had them hot like the sun. They knew there would be hell to pay for Cash having to fight, when he paid them to lay shit down that was hostile or unfriendly.

He got off the ground and dusted of his clothes. Martez felt the cut under his eye and saw Cash's mouth and nose bleeding. For a moment, Cash wish he had his pistol on him to blow Martez's brains everywhere. But the thought only lasted a second, because even though they weren't best friends, they were still guys at the end of the day. A fight wouldn't change that. Never had, never would. Martez walked over to Cash as Reese held team savage at gun point and they shook up before hugging each other like old times.

When Reese put his gun away everyone jumped up and pulled their hammers.

"It's too late now, y'all gotta step it up. We all could've got hit if bro wasn't the guys. So, put them tools up while I talk to skud em," Cash said, disappointed in them. It upset him they let someone get the ups on him. He smiled, pondering how long it's been since he threw hands.

When they were kids, all their disagreements ended in blows. But as they got older, they learned to respect each other, everyone but him and Martez. He'd been getting away with disrespecting Martez for years, which made him forget he was from the mud just like him. He was a street nigga before a lawyer. Martez wasn't a hoe by any means, and today he gained Cash's respect once again.

Reese pulled a pre-rolled blunt from his pocket and flamed it up. The old companions sat back and talked out their differences for an hour, before Martez told them he was going home.

After dropping Reese off he went in the house and called Bee's name, but she didn't answer.

He called her again, still no answer. Once he made it to their bedroom his heart dropped. The room was a mess, their things were everywhere. On the dresser he found a letter. He picked it up and began reading.

Martez, you are my one and only love, without you I don't know where I'd be. You opened my eyes to a life I never knew existed. You gave love to a lost soul and showed me the way. You are a wonderful person, a person too good for me. I would hate to have anything happen to you. So, I must leave. You won't understand it, but god finds a way to destroy everything I treasure.

But I won't let him slaughter you. I love you with all my heart, you're the only man I have ever wanted. So, believe me when I say this is the most difficult decision of my life. I'm sorry, but I must leave to save you. I want you to know that my heart will always belong to you.

Love,

Bee

He felt weak and couldn't understand why she left. In their whole relationship, they never fought once. He thought they were happy. How could she do him like this?

His mind began to play tricks on him, and he began to second guess their love. *"Damn,"* he said, out loud. *"Did she even love me?"* he thought while letting the letter fall from his hands and onto the floor alone with a single tear.

ACE BOOGIE

CHAPTER THIRTEEN

Two Weeks Later

*c*ash and Black rolled round Chicago and sipped on purple drink. The pain from the loss was still agonizing, but she kept her emotions intact. She still hadn't talked to Bee, which hurt a lot. She lost one sister to the game and another one to the pain of that loss.

It was her fault Glory was gone, at least that's what she believed. But Cash broke it down to her from his perspective. He explained that if she was there, she'd be the one dead. When he laid it out that way, it eased her pain and made her thankful to be alive.

"A, ma I'm feeling you, so I ain't gone lie to you. If you gone be with me, you gotta be a part of the team. I got mad love for you, but I ain't a one-woman man...I got four Bitch's who stay in one of my mansions. If you wanna be with me, you gotta be with them."

This new revelation smacked her in the face. She didn't know what to say, she didn't like women. She never had a bisexual moment or thought about being with a woman. "Why are you just now telling me this?" she asked, confused. Things between them seemed to be going well. He slept with her almost every night. When did he have time for these bitches he was talking about? If he was able to stay with her all night, what kind of relationship did they have?

Cash rubbed his hand over this face before answering. "I wasn't sure we had something, so I wasn't gone just bring any woman home to meet the loves of my life. I know this all might sound crazy, and that's because it is. But I'll make sure you are conformable and loved at the same time. You won't want for anything. I'll show you respect, and so will they. There won't be any fighting," he said.

Black took in everything he said. It sounded good to a young, lost girl. Maybe it was her broken heart or the lean that had her feeling like Y.O.L.O., so she said, "fuck it, why not." In this moment, what did she have to lose?

"I'll try it once, and if I don't like it, what happens to us?" she asked, already hooked on him. Her mind wasn't developed enough to be with an older man, neither was her body. Everything about him was too advanced for her. He smiled knowing that once his girls got their hands on her, she'd never be the same.

"If you don't like it, you'll never have to do it again," he said, pulling up to the house where Dria, Barbie, Lavish, and Lisa stayed. They were sister wives. Black was nervous when she entered the house. She followed Cash to the living room where she saw 4 knockout, beautiful, naked women.

At the sight of the naked woman, she knew Cash had this planned long before informing her. She glanced at Cash; he had a big smile on his face.

"Damn daddy she looks like she just turned 18…But she cute though. I like the dreads," Dria said, walking to her. Black watched Dria's beautiful body as she walked towards her. She stared at her lovely full breast and firm nipples.

"You can touch them," Dria whispered. Without thinking, Black's hands moved with a mind of their own and begin to caress her breast.

"Mm mm," Dria moaned.

There was something mesmerizing about massaging her smooth, large mounds. Black's were smaller but feeling Dria's was a new guilty pleasure.

"I think everyone is enjoying the show," Dria said. Black glanced over in was shocked by everyone playing with themselves. Cash was in the loveseat with his large erection, slowly massaging it. Dria pulled her close and kissed her. She felt her tongue begin to play in her mouth and felt her hard nipples brush against her chest.

Nervousness was starting to give away to fantasy and raw lust. Dria helped her undress, before kissing her way from her ear down to her neck. She massaged her breasts then replaced her hands with her lips. Black spread her legs as Dria slid down her body. The feeling of a woman licking her nipples was incredible. Dria was licking and sucking on her left breast, when Cash joined in. They continued to suck her nipples, before turning to kiss each other while still playing with her tits. They resumed kissing her body, but Dria headed south. She felt her kisses move pass her naval, and over her hip bone, then down her thigh. The feeling made her feel like she was flying. Dria begin licking her inner thigh, then slowly licked her pussy.

It was like nothing she'd ever felt before. Dria ate her like she knew exactly what she needed. She tongued Black for a few minutes, then pushed her tongue inside her. After doing this, she moved up to her clit and licked it just the right way.

She was about to cum when Cash stopped kissing her and rolled onto his back. She lifted her head and saw Dria's face between her legs, while she held Cash's dick in her hand. Shy, modest Black let out a loud cry while having a crushing orgasm. The sight of them took her over the edge. She opened her eyes to see Barbie strapping on a 10-inch dildo. She positioned the strap-on between Lavish's legs, as Lisa straddled Black's virgin face. She was so turned on she didn't think twice about eating pussy for the first time.

They continued like this for hours...fucking, sucking, and just like that, Black was turned on. If Bee knew what she was up to she'd go crazy, Black thought. But then again, she didn't care anymore, so why should she?

*****

"I'll see you next week," Bee said to one of her regular customers. She closed the door to her hotel room and placed the 9.mm on the bed. She held the pistol in her hand throughout the whole transaction.

She was nervous doing business alone, but she could handle herself. If she even thought something was going to go wrong, she'd leave a body in the room before making her exit. Bee pulled out the duffle bag and began counting the money. After she left Martez's house, she called Ryan to pay him his money. Then, she had him front her 500 pounds. She went to Glory's house, got her savings, and placed it in a safety deposit box.

After two weeks of hard trapping, she had 300 bands inside the room with her. Bee knew it wasn't smart to make moves outta the same spot she kept her bag, but her mind wasn't functioning correctly. Her heart was shattered. She'd lost her only friends, along with her man in a matter of weeks.

She was afraid and left the love of her life. She was scared that he'd end up like everything else she held dear. Her life was crazy like that, as long as she could remember, bad things happened to the people around her. She really hoped he understood why she left, but a part of her knew he wouldn't.

Once she had time to ponder her decision to leave, she regretted it. It was the worst decision of her life. She wanted to run back to him in beg for forgiveness. She wanted to tell him that she'd never leave again.

But it was too late to say sorry. Her mistake might've made him feel her love was unrighteous, maybe even unjust.

He was a good man and she repaid him by abandoning him outta fear. She'd been selfish, only thinking about her feelings and not how they affected him. Why would he take her back? She made up her mind to stay away from him, her pride was standing in the way of her true love. Bee wiped the tears from her eyes and finished counting the money. After making sure her money added up, she stood to pack her things. It was time to exit this hotel. She'd stayed long enough. The last two weeks, it was all she saw. When she was hungry, she ordered room service. She did everything she could to avoid going outside.

Madison was a small city, so she stayed inside to avoid bumping into Martez. She didn't wanna take that chance until her heart was healed. Thinking about him reminded her of the last time they saw each other and how Cash put his hands on her. Her pride wouldn't let him get away with it. The troubled soul inside her wanted to unleash some pain from losing Glory.

What better way to do it then murder?

The loss turned her into a savage. She wanted to see red everywhere on Cash like a steak when it's raw. The day she caught her first body made her heartless. She could kill without remorse. Taking a life is what she planned to do. She was gone take his last breath away. She put the last pair of pants in her bag before exiting the room. It would all begin at what was advertised as the party of the year. Cash was having a blowout at Q.O.H. in Milwaukee tonight, where she planned to take his life.

(Tre Boi)

Tre Boi was at home. He'd spent the last few weeks going behind Cash and June's backs, murdering opps without remorse. He felt it had to be done; he couldn't let someone kill children in his hood without consequences.

Even though he understood Cash was trying to look out for them now, who was gone look out for the people who lost their lives. Tre Boi felt like the Army's rule, "no man left behind." To him, no murder would go unanswered. You kill one of his, he killed three of yours.

His iPhone rang on the couch next to him. When he picked it up, he saw it was an unknown number but decided to answer anyways.

"Who this?" he asked.

"Kia," she replied, sounding nervous. She was a little ashamed to be calling him after he never gave her a ring. But she needed some good dick, and she wanted it now.

"Damn my bad for never calling, I had a lot going on," he said sincerely.

"I'm not ya bitch! You ain't gotta explain nothing to me," she said.

"I see so what's to it, you looking to get dick down again?" he asked, smiling from ear to ear, cause he knew she was.

"You know what I want. So, can you give it to me?" she asked in an almost pleading voice.

"I'm going to this party tonight in Milwaukee, so I don't know. If you want, you can meet me there then we can do us afterwards," he said.

"Boi what you know about my city?" she questioned.

"My big hommie own a club out there, and he throwing a big party...So, you gone show up or what?"

"Where is it at?" she asked.

"Some place called Q.O.H! If you don't know where it's at, I'll give you the info to plug in your GPS," he said, leaning back and lighting up a blunt.

Kia's heart dropped when she heard the name of the club she'd once stripped at, and that her ex-lovers use to own.

"You still there?" Tre Boi asked once she didn't respond.

"Ya," Kia said. "I know where it's at. I'll meet you there," she added.

"Cool, cool. See you tonight," Tre Boi said before hanging up the phone.

(Kia)

Kia placed the phone on the bed as her head spun. The world was a small place. What was the chance life would lead her back to the place it all began?

She thought about cancelling her date with Tre Boi. She was scared of the memories Q.O.H. would bring back. Her life had moved forward, and that place could unravel it all. She closed her eyes and rubbed her hands over her face slowly. When she opened them, her mind was made up. She'd go there tonight and face her fears. Her phone rang, bringing her back to reality. When she picked it up, she saw it was Danjunema.

"Hi baby," she answered.

"Call to talk to you for a second. What you doing?" he asked, excited to hear her voice.

"Nothing daddy! Just thinking of you and laying in bed," she lied, feeling a little guilty. "When you coming home?" she added.

"In a week or two. I got a little more business to handle," he responded. A tear escaped her eyes, she really missed him despite her cheating.

"I need you here daddy!" she cried. Danjunema heard the tears and pain in her voice, and it touched his heart to know she missed him.

"I need to be there. I'll be home soon," he said, hoping to comfort her. "Don't worry, we'll be together before you know it," he added. Kia wiped the tears away from her eyes and pulled herself together. "OK daddy come home soon," she said.

"OK I'll be right there!" Danjunema yelled to someone and his background.

"I gotta go baby!" he said, a little disappointed.

"OK I love ya," she said before ending the call, and laying back and bed. She had so much on her mind, she could barely think. She was in love, and at the same time, she was about to go fuck another man. Her life was all over the place and she didn't know where it was headed. She prayed to god to take all these thoughts and allow her to enjoy herself tonight.

(Chicago)

June and Cash sat in his mansion. When June walked in, he saw five gorgeous eye-catching women sleeping in a king size bed together. It didn't take the most intelligent person in the world to know what had taken place before he arrived.

He glanced around the house. It was nice, but he'd seen nicer ones that Cash owned. They sat in his office engaging in a business conversation.

"OK so you said once every 6 months I meet you, pick up the work, and then meet the team to distribute it?" June asked.

"That's it that's all. I only need you to do this once while I find out who killed my twin brother. It won't take long cuz the way I'm about to turn Wisconsin upside-down nigga gone be bagging to give me the information I'm looking for. After tonight, I'm done partying, hustling, and even fucking until I find out who got my brother's body under, they belt."

"Why you choosing me? Why you trusting me with all this?" June asked. He never thought Cash trusted him much.

"Because you a king waiting to be crowned, that's why. When I'm gone, you next up," Cash smiled.

He knew when he left the game his kingdom would be in good hands. His statement made June feel horrible about planning to snake him.

"That means a lot coming from you skud," June said sincerely. He began to regret his disloyalty. Since the loss of his brother, Cash changed a lot. It seemed he wanted everybody he cared about to know he loved them.

"No homo, I love you lil bro. You the only nigga. on the team, I trust," Cash added.

"I got you big bro, no lie, everything gone be good in my hands, don't worry," June said, standing up to leave.

They shook up and Cash walked him to the door. On the way out, June looked in the bedroom and saw a woman with locks in her face between another's legs. Cash stopped in the doorway. "Black you want me to take you home, or you staying?" he joked, already knowing the answer.

She lifted her head from Dria's lap, "I'm staying."

Cash smiled and continued walking June to the door.

"You in this bitch living like a pimp," June joked.

"Nah, I love them bitches in that room. They my heart...A pimp feels nothing for his hoes. I do, that's the difference. I choose to have all mine in one house. I ain't gone lie and be fighting with them about each other. It's better to be open and let them get to know one another on a personal level..." Cash said while opening the door for June to leave.

He smiled at his big hommie before walking out and letting Cash have the last word. He got in his Mercedes Benz C-class, and kissed Kim before they pulled off. *She was the only woman he needed,* he thought, picking up a blunt she rolled while he was inside.

(One Hour Later)

Martez spent the last two weeks searching for Bee but had no luck. He had another way to find her but didn't wanna invade her privacy. His heart was demolished without her.

He thought they were in love; how could she pick up and leave him sick like that. He tried getting over her but deep down he knew he never would. He planned to move on with his life, because if she really loved him, she knew where to find him. He stepped outta the shower before drying off and heading to his room to pick an outfit out for the Bag Team party. He was only attending to show love to Cash and his team. After throwing hands, their relationship had improved. It felt good to go around him without feeling some type of way.

Even though he didn't like the way Cash moved in the game or didn't like hanging with him all the time, tonight was different. He wanted to show out a little bit. He was looking forward to spending some of his hard-earned savings. He glanced at his two shoes for tonight. The two Gucci fits on the bed, had him debating witch one to wear. He wanted to be the flyest nigga in the building. He was try'na get some pussy to get his mind off Bee. Shit, she wasn't thinking about him, or she would've come home already. His phone vibrated on the nightstand, and he walked over and answered it.

"What good skud," he said to Reese.

"Shit nigga, when the fuck you coming to get me?"

"Broski I ain't even dressed yet."

"Fuck you mean you ain't dressed????? Come on with that fake ass Odell Beckham Jr. shit. You ain't gotta be the last nigga to the party," Reese joked, and they shared a laugh.

"I'm almost ready skud, no lie," he casually said.

"Come the fuck on, shit by the time we get there, Cash's team gone be done fucking all the bitches."

Martez laughed at his friend before hanging up the phone. He closed his eyes and threw the line on the bed to pick his outfit. It landed on the red and white Gucci pants.

*****

Kia stepped into Q.O.H. on the arm of Tre Boi; they'd met in the parking lot before entering. Things were crazy inside and it was packed wall to wall. She felt strange being inside the club without being able to see Angel running the place. But the drinks she'd consumed before coming had her feeling a little mellow.

She glanced over at her man for the night and smiled. He was her type of nigga. She looked at his Burberry shirt and Fendi pants, which he looked nice in, but his Rolex set his outfit off.

"What you smiling at?" he yelled over the music.

"You, is that alright? Or do I gotta pay for that too?" she joked.

"Nah, tonight everything free!" he said.

"Who said I want it for free? That 30 bands was light. I'm really enjoying our little game," she said. Tre Boi laughed, "Yo ass crazy.... But talk that shit then! I'm kind of into that anyways," he said. It was Kia's turn to laugh now. "Crazy?? This wouldn't be the first time I was called that," she responded, only half joking.

A man approached them that made Kia's mouth fall open. She felt like she was staring at a ghost. Cash walked up and shook Tre Boi's hand. It was like looking into the eyes of Money all over. His twin would always be a reminder of his presence on this earth.

"What's good boi boi?" Cash asked.

"Shit skud coming to celebrate with ya," Tre Boi responded.

"Who this?" Cash asked, starring at Kia.

"Oh, my bad skud, this my friend Kia. Kia, this my nigga Cash," Tre Boi said introducing them. Cash put his hand out for her to shake and she took it. Once they released each other, Cash got a feeling he'd already met this woman before.

"Don't I know you from somewhere?" he asked.

"I don't think so," she lied, as her mind flashed back to the day she saw him while with Money. "Well imma get a drink and leave y'all to have a conversation," she said in a rush to escape before he remembered where he knew her from.

"OK ma, I'll be over there and a second," Tre Boi said. Kia walked over to the bar and took a seat next to a stunning red head, who seem to have a lot on her mind. She didn't even look up when Kia took a seat next to her.

Kia quickly placed an order and received her drink just a fast as she ordered it. She downed the drink before she saw a flash of what looked like a pistol in the hand of the red head under the table. But when she looked, there was nothing in sight, so she blamed the illusion on the liquor. When she looked at Tre Boi, he was still conversating with Cash, and she wondered how they knew each other. She planned on asking him before the end of the night.

*****

An hour later, Martez and Reese pulled up to Q.O.H. in his Range Rover. The party was already under way by the time they arrived. There was still a line a block long. Reese called Cash and informed him they were outside.

Five minutes later, a bodyguard came to escort them inside. It was packed and women out numbered men 5 to 1.

The only men in attendance were the Bagz of Money Gang, Team Savage, and a few D-boys from Madison, Beloit, and

Chicago. They pushed their way to the stage, where Cash and the team was making it rain as they dance to Moody' latest hit.

"What's good skud?" Cash yelled over the music and they shook up. Martez looked around the club Money and his wife Angel built before they were murdered. They really did a good job. Cash bought it to keep his twin's memory alive.

"Shit my nigga try'na get like you," Reese yelled. Cash threw his hands in the air.

"All this is mine...And everything I got, my bros got. We run this city and this whole state. Before it's all said and done, we gone run the world," Cash said feeling the liquor and his self. He was a born king and a born leader. Reese smiled, knowing better then to interrupt Cash while jacking.

One of Future hits poured through the speaker and the club went insane. Cash walked over to a bunch of people before pulling out a stack of hundreds from his LV bag. As Future did his thing, Cash begin to make it rain.

International we taking over all the countries

And nationality they coming baby the coming

Ride shotgun in the foreign that's a Rover

Until you gunned down, we gone never have closure

Got real estate downtown we investing all over

I heard you try'na talk down like we I ain't focused

I know you try'na play around like I ain't got soldiers.

Martez looked on as Cash put on a show. He was built for the spotlight. The smile on his face said it all. A slim woman with a plump ass passed by him and got his attention, reminding him of the reason he'd come out. He approached her. "A ma, what's yo name," he asked.

She turned around and saw him in front of her, making her mouth water. She was fucking him tonight."Ke Ke," she said in a sexy voice.

*****

Bee was settled at the bar in full disguise. As she watched Martez whispering in a woman's ear., the red wig and dark makeup concealed her identity. She was unrecognizable.

She went between watching the party and her ex-lover. It broke her heart seeing him with another woman, but now wasn't the time to act like a bitch. She was on a mission and plans needed to be followed.

She clenched her savages with both hands under the table. She concealed them entering the club while the security guard was busy getting a free feel to check her properly.

She strolled up to the stage, where Cash stood on a table throwing money. After positioning herself in front of him, he began to make it poor hundreds on her. This only enraged her more. *Who the fuck did he think he was to put his hands on her*? she thought. Now he was throwing money on her like she was a whore. It only took a second to pull her 9.mm and aim.

Cash's eyes widened at the sight of the pistols. His life flashed before his eyes. The first thing he saw was his family when he was young, and the good times when he got alone with his twin. He saw his mother crying and the promises he made. No, he couldn't die tonight, he thought as he tried getting outta the way, but it was too late.

Boc! Boc! Boc! Boc! Boc!

The first two bullets hammered into his chest, sending him slamming to the ground as the others hit bystanders. People scrambled to get outta the path of the gunfire.

Bee aimed again at Cash's body laying on the floor. She stared at him and didn't see fear in his eyes. In fact, he was smiling at her. Blood from his chest wounds sputtered onto his face. He looked at peace for a man about to die.

Boc! Boc! Boc! Boc! Boc! Boc! Boc! Boc! Boc!

She pumped his body full of bullets. Members of team savage tried figuring out where the gunshots were coming from but were unsuccessful. All the people running around made it impossible, as they pushed each other over try'na make it to the exit...

Bee stared at Cash's body in a pool of blood and smiled, before blending in with the pandemonium exiting the club. Once she was outside, she stopped running and walked to her car with a big smile on her face. She was so happy it turned her on. It felt like her trigger finger was connected to her clit. Bee got in the car and took a deep breath. For a person who just committed murder, she wasn't in a rush. She watched as people jumped in their cars, before speeding out the parking lot. She turned on some music before slowly pulling off. When she turned out the lot, she saw Martez and Reese carrying a body outta the club.

Could he still be alive, she wondered, but quickly dismissed the thought. He been hit too many times.

She turned up "EAT" by Young MA.

Nobody safe anymore,

Had to wake you niggaz up, I couldn't wait anymore.

She lip sing along as she made a safe getaway. Thoughts of Martez whispering in the lady's ear broke her heart. It hurt to see him over her so soon. She thought about the two weeks she spent laid up sick, while he was more than likely somewhere fucking.

A tear escaped as the pain set in. She felt slow for letting herself fall in love. She saw this story a million times and knew the ending. But it looked a lot less painful from the outside looking in. Now that she was heartbroken herself, she understood the tears she'd seen women shedding.

She wiped her eyes and thought about where her life was heading. With no friends, no man, and no family she was all alone, but she wasn't broke. A customer had just placed an order for 100 pounds. Now that Cash was out the way, she could focus on this bag. With revenge on Cash, she only needed June. Then, her sister could rest in peace.

One more body wouldn't hurt, she told herself. After he was gone, she'd retire her Pretty Savages.

(An Hour Later)

Martez, Reese, Black, Dria, Barbie, Lesa, Lavish, June, Kim, and 30 members of Team Savage packed the hospital's waiting room. Everyone was lost in their own thoughts. They wondered if Cash would make it. He'd been shot 11 times, most of them to his core.

He also lost a lot of blood on the ride to the hospital. Martez didn't see how he could survive all them gunshots, but prayed he was wrong. He looked down at his hands that were stained with his friend's blood.

It all happened so fast. One minute they are partying, the next shots rang out. Once they ended, he found Cash laying in his own blood.

Damn! Life was so unpredictable. Moments like this made him glad that he only did business with one person. He didn't have enemies or haters try'na get him out the way to succeed on their own. When you played the game full time, any moment a bullet could come flying with yo name on it.

As powerful as Cash was, he wasn't exempt, and a bullet could end it all.

Martez looked at Reese with his head down, and wondered what thoughts were running through his mind.

The doctor came out and everyone stood to their feet waiting to hear bad news.

"I got some good news in bad news...he's stable but has to have a few more surgeries. We are confident he will make a full recovery. I want you all to know he is a lucky man...And god was with him tonight," the doctor said. He waited a moment, but once no one responded, he walked away assuming they were at a loss for words. It was nothing new to him, different families acted in different ways.

They all began to hug each other and shake up, fortunate to hear the news. Martez walked over in hugged Reese.

"Imma head home, call me when he outta surgery, "he said.

"I got ya skud," Reese replied and they shook up. He was on his way out the door when Black stopped him.

"Can I speak with you?" she asked.

"Ya what's good?"

Black thought about whether to share this information with him. She was scared he'd tell Bee. She was worried about Bee; she was losing it. When she heard a woman shot Cash, it only took a second to come to the conclusion Bee was responsible.

"This has to stay between us. I need yo word, what imma bout to tell you won't come back on me."

Martez saw how scared she was and gave his word.

"I know who shot Cash."

"Who?" he asked.

"Bee...I know you might think she's not capable of this, but she has already killed two people," she whispered. He couldn't believe what he'd just heard. Not his Bee, not his woman. It wasn't possible.

She wasn't a murderer. "Who all you told this too?" he asked, grabbing her arm and pulling her close.

"Nobody, just you. I don't want nothing to happen to her. She still my sister no matter what happens between us," she responded while pulling her arm away.

"That's good to hear, you know this could get her killed."

"That's why I'm only telling you. If she did this, she need yo help. You need to find her and make her stop this madness," she pleaded.

"I will, but never repeat this conversation," he said walking out the door.

On his ride home, he thought about the information Black shared with him. What if Bee was the shooter? If it was her, she was in over her head. He had to find her to make sure she wasn't responsible. Beefing with Cash would get outta hand. He didn't have a problem putting a check on a muthafucka's head. If anything happened to Bee, he wouldn't be able to live with himself.

He needed to find her before Cash got outta surgery.

Martez pulled into his parking lot and parked his car before picking up his phone and dialing his private investigator. She was the best PI in the state of Wisconsin.

"Hi Martez, how may I help you?" the PI asked.

"I need to find someone ASAP," he said.

"Name and phone number?" she asked, knowing he knew the process. He gave her Bee's information before hanging up. He stayed in the car, knowing it wouldn't take long to get a location.

(Meanwhile)

Bee went to the nearest hospital right after the shooting, wanting to make sure Cash was gone. It wasn't long until she saw a van pull up to the emergency room calling for help. She watched as staff rushed to get Cash inside. *Damn he got heart*, she laughed.

She wasn't even mad. A minute later, she watched Glory's murderer step outta a car and run inside along with his accomplice.

God could be good at times, she thought before parking and waiting on them to come out. A part of her wanted to wait for a better time to make her move, but the pain inside wasn't having it.

About 20 minutes went by before she saw Black pull up with a group of women. At that moment, she knew Cash was still alive.

But she was no longer concerned with him. She was out to avenge her sister's murder, not his disrespect. She wondered how they all knew one another.

She sat and thought about all kinds of things for over an hour as she waited. It hurt to watch Martez leave and not talk to him. But she had more important things to take care of. After Martez pulled out the lot, Black and the group of women left as well. Then, about two minute later, June and Kim exited the building along with a group of men. Bee watched as the guy she'd saw talking to Cash at the club pulled up and walked over to them followed by a woman.

Damn, she thought. There was too many of them to make a move tonight.

"Nah fuck that," she said while turning the car on. She slowly pulled to the emergency room where they stood and rolled the window down. No one seemed to notice her.

*****

June was on his phone talking to Kutta, when he was shoved to the ground, before shots were fired.

Boc! Boc! Boc! Boc! Boc! Boc! Boc! Boc!

They all ran for cover until the shots stopped. Once they did, TDN gave chase.

Boom! Boom! Boom! Boom!

June watched from the ground, but TDN was unable to hit the driver as the van got away. He stood to his feet with everyone but Tre Boi and Kim. He looked at the love of his life, his backbone. She was holding her chest where 3 rounds knocked her to the pavement. June dropped to his knees and held her as emergency stuff rushed to help the falling.

She stared into his eyes, "Don't cry daddy, I'm OK, I saved you, like you saved me."

June rubbed his hands over her face. He held back tears in his eyes and paid no attention to the commotion going on around him. The only thing that seemed to matter was the love of his life. The world seemed to come to a standstill as he stared into her eyes.

"The shooter was the girl from the robbery, daddy. The one who came down the stairs," she said, coughing up blood. The staff asked him to move, so they could attend to her, but he'd shot enough people to know she wouldn't make it.

"I love you ma," he said as they put her on a stretcher.

"Love ya too," she said, before passing out. They rushed her away. June looked over and saw a woman holding Tre Boi's dead body. He had a single gunshot wound to the head. June didn't even notice he was crying. He'd just lost another hommie, and his wifey more than likely wouldn't make it. He wiped the tears away just as the woman glanced up at him. They stared at one another. Kia saw the rage in his eyes as he snatched her up by her hair, pulling her away from Tre Boi's body. He pulled his pistol from his pocket and pointed it at her forehead just as TDN came running back. Everyone watched June wondering what he was doing.

"You had something to do with this didn't you?" he asked, without any reason to believe she did.

He was looking for someone to blame and she was the closest one. "No, I didn't," she said mugging him. June stared into her eyes before pulling the pistol away and allowing her to stand.

"You coming with me!" he said finally while about to rob her.

"No, I ain't!" she said pointing over his shoulders. The crowd glanced back and saw 5 Africans holding AK47s pointed at them. "Maybe next time," she said, laughing at how she always seemed to have the upper hand. "Sorry about your friend, he really knew how to fuck... May that D rest in Peace," she joked, not giving two fucks about Tre Boi. June and his team stood there frozen, praying they wouldn't be left out there on the pavement. June watched as Kia took the phone off one of the Africans and threw it to him. He caught it.

"What's this for?" he yelled enraged. "Business, I'll give you a call," she said stepping into a minivan as her team slowly loaded in behind her while keeping them at gunpoint. Once they were all safely inside, they sped away.

CHAPTER FOURTEEN

*B*ee woke up at 4am to a knock on the hotel door. She grabbed one of her savages before looking out the peephole and saw Martez. Her heart dropped. *What is he doing here,* she thought? *How did he know where to find me?* she questioned. Her mind ran wild as she ran to hide the red wig under the bed.

Once it was put away, she opened the door with her gun still in hand, unaware of what he knew. She opened it in boy shorts and a bra.

Martez grabbed her around the neck the moment the door open, thrusting her into the wall at the back of the room. It happens so quick she wasn't able to react fast enough.

"Why?" he yelled with spit flying from his mouth and landing on her face.

"Why what Martez?" she asked, unable to breathe.

"Why the fuck you try killing my nigga?"

"I don't know what you talking about," she lied. "But if you don't get yo fucking hands off me, imma kill you," she added, putting the 9.mm to his chest.

He peeked down at the firearm pointed at his heart. "You gone shoot me to?" he questioned.

She stared into his eyes and saw the man of her dreams; she couldn't pull the trigger if she wanted to. But he didn't know that, so she continued to act tough.

He saw through her fake toughness before releasing her.

They looked into one another's eyes for a moment, before Bee stood on her tiptoes and kissed his lips which he returned with passion. Martez felt weak for kissing her. But he needed to be inside her. She always felt so good. Bee places the gun on the nightstand as he picked her up. She wrapped her legs around him, and he placed her on the bed. She sat up to remove his belt, unable to wait to hold his dick in her hands.

Martez stared down at her while she took his manhood in her mouth. He pulled his cock away from her after only a few seconds. He undressed her before she laid back on the bed. Dropping to his knees, he pressed his face into her pussy. His tongue flicked out and touched her clit. His warm breath and wet tongue aroused her greatly.

She gasped as he parted her nether lips then bought his mouth to her waiting pussy. She leaned her head back and closed her eyes, but he wasn't having none of that.

"Look at me," he whispered, and she automatically obeyed his command. She stared at him as he continued to treat her to an amazing feeling.

He parted her lips so wide she felt an ache deep within herself, a hunger that made her crave everything he had to give. He brought his mouth directly to her clit, ringing it with his lips while his tongue expertly stroked it again and again.

She squirmed and moaned reveling in every sensation. He knew exactly how to touch her. He teased her by running his tongue around her clit; he spiraled it with pleasure. She didn't sense it before it happened, but all of a sudden, she was cumming—hard and furiously, bucking against his mouth as she did. He continued to lick her clit as if it was a piece of candy.

*****

An hour later, Bee was asleep. They hadn't talked about the elephant in the room. Martez laid in bed with mixed emotions. After sex, she went to take a shower, and once she was in, he searched the room and found the red wig under the bed. She interrupted his search and he wasn't able to put it back. It laid on the chair in the room when she got in bed. He wondered if she noticed it or not. He was in deep thought about his emotions, cause a part of him wanted to remain loyal to his childhood friend. On the other hand, he was in love with the enemy. Not even 24 hours ago, she tried killing his people, and here he was laying with her. Bee rolled over and threw her arm around him.

"You ok daddy?" she asked, cause he seemed to have a lot on his mind. The way he was staring into space was a dead giveaway. She glanced over and saw the wig on the chair and her heart skipped a beat.

Why lord? she thought. Why did he always make things difficult on her?

"You never answered my question. Why did you try killing my nigga?" Martez said, taking her away from her thoughts.

"What friend, Martez? I don't know who you talking bout."

"You gone lie to me like that? Damn ma, I thought we was better than that. You know who the fuck I'm talking about. You tried killing my nigga, Cash."

"I didn't shoot him Martez, I would never lie to you about anything," she said, looking into his eyes. She was a convincing liar. If he hadn't seen the wig himself, he would've believed it. "I never said he got shot," he said. "How you know that?" he continued. Bee shot back without thinking, "It don't take a rocket scientist to come to the conclusion that a drug dealer could get shot. It was just a lucky guess Martez," she said with her face skewed up.

"I would never make you choose between me and yo friends. I love you baby and won't hurt you...Now turn around and let me give you a massage," she said in a sweet voice. Against his better judgement he turned over and she mounted his back. She slowly began massaging his neck in shoulders.

Tears ran down her face. The decision she'd made a moment ago was to blame. She stared over at the 9.mm on the nightstand as she continued to work on his back.

It had to be done, but that wouldn't stop the tears from flowing. This would hurt her forever. Pulling the trigger would bring her to the brake of death. Living without him for a few weeks felt like hell, so she couldn't imagine what a lifetime would feel like. She was signing her own death certificate, because without him, she was as good as dead.

When she lied a moment ago, a hateful unpleasant expression flashed across his face. He would betray her, she knew it. It was only a matter of time. The hate would only manifest and outweigh the love. She reached over and picked up the gun to murder the love of her life. But the instant she felt the weight of the cold steel, it hit her like a ton of bricks. The room was registered in her real name. She couldn't kill him here; the police would be searching for her in the morning if she did. She slowly removed her hand from the firearm and took a deep breath. Tomorrow she'd take care of him in a place that didn't lead back to her. But tonight, she'd spend time with him and make love.

CHAPTER FIFTHTEEN

*M*artez pretended to sleep the rest of the night before leaving first thing in the morning. He didn't wake Bee or say goodbye. He thought about last night's massage. The moment she took her hand off him, he regretted trusting her behind him. She didn't know that he noticed her contemplating whether to kill him or not. When he heard the steel hit the nightstand, he let out a deep breath. He didn't know why she didn't pull the trigger, maybe it was cause she loved him. But he knew it had something to do with the room being in her name.

If it hadn't been the PI, he wouldn't have been able to locate her. He got in his Range Rover, thankful to be alive before pulling off. He couldn't trust Bee now that she tried killing him and didn't want to spend the rest of his life looking over his shoulders for the moment she'd strike like a lioness. *Damn, love was a bitch!*

(Meanwhile)

June sat inside Boo Boo's car with gloves on and pistol out. After he got the news Kim died, he went looking for the bitch responsible. Boo Boo put him on the lick, so he was to blame.

"What else you know about these hoes?" he questioned.

Boo Boo was scared to death, he knew about June's background. He'd heard how he killed without regret. The streets said he had over 50 bodies, but he saw the stars for himself. The last he knew, it was 13.

"I told you everything I know already... We got into it when I grabbed the other bitch around the neck. I was finna take the pounds, when the other one came out the bathroom holding two hammers and robbed me. That's all I know, other than the phone number."

He said try'na save his life. June pointed his gun in his face. "You sure that's all you know? You better think before you never think again."

"One had long dreadlocks, I think the other one called her Black," he said, pleading for his life. *Black, that's Cash's new bitch name, and she got locks to, it has to be the same person.* He wondered if it was before putting a bullet through Boo Boo's head.

Boc!

Hopefully he had the right person, because if not, he would search the world until he found her murderer.

Boc! Boc!

He shot Boo Boo's dead body two more times before existing the car. He was done playing, it was time for action.

(Meanwhile)

Bee received a text from Martez about needing to see her tonight. She laughed at how men let pussy control their heart once they were in love. She drove to her old apartment to get a few things. She kept the apartment in case they needed a place to stay, and because it was their first real home. Tonight, she was gone murder Martez before leaving town.

She got out and went inside. The moment she entered, it felt like her world changed. Gone was the cold-blooded killer, in her place stood a loving friend. Tears rolled down her face. Her life was a mess, a dark hole, and a blood bath.

But for what reason? The love of money! She'd gained the world and lost it all over night. When she lost her friends, it felt useless.

The apartment reminded her of a better time. She reminisced about the happy times they shared. She closed her eyes and saw Black and Glory, smiling, laughing, and even crying. She saw her world before the drugs, revenge, and murders.

She opened her eyes once those happy members were replaced with the vision of Glory's dead body in her arms. Life was great until that night. She thought the curse that lingered over her was broken until that night.

But she'd mistaken. She wished they never run away. If they hadn't, Glory would still be alive. They would've been safer with a ra\per, than in the streets with a leader who was new to the game. She walked out the apartment without taking a thing, leaving it the way they left it. She got back in her car and pulled off with no set destination. It pained her to wait until nightfall to release some stress. Killing Martez would hurt, at the same time, it would set her free. It would bring an adrenaline rush out of this world. When she pulled the trigger, it felt like an orgasm. She smiled at how crazy it was to be fantasizing about killing her one true love.

If there was ever a question in her mind, she was heartless. It was answered now. Looking in the review mirror, she saw her reflection didn't match her heart. When you saw her, the last thing you saw was a coldblooded killer. She'd been battling the devil from the day she was born. He wanted her soul as long as she could remember, and now, he had it. Once Martez was gone, she'd be alone with the undertaker.

*****

June, Kutta, and Bullet waited for one of Cash's girls to answer the door. The moment it opened, June shot Lavish in the face, killing her on impact. Her body hit the ground like a ton of bricks. Bullet and Kutta rushed the house to find the remaining woman.

June slowly stepped over Lavish's dead body. His mind was on auto pilot. He'd done this enough times to do it without thinking.

Boc! Boc! Boc! Boc!

He heard 4 shots upstairs along with a loud scream. A moment later, Bullet dragged Black down the stairs by her locks. June smiled thinking about how close he was to finding Kim's murderer.

"Wait, please don't kill me," Black cried.

"Imma ask you this once, where yo friend at? The bitch with two pistols," June asked placing his weapon to her forehead.

"I don't know where she at. Martez said he was gone find her," she said crying.

"Martez? Cash's guy Martez?" June asked.

"Ya she his girlfriend." June looked at the beautiful young woman on her knees in front of him. She was a masterpiece, made by god. The artwork was to wonderful to destroy, nah he had better plans for her.

"Imma give you two options, the first is to die here with the rest of them. The second is to come with me," he said. She didn't know what to think. Was he gone rape her? The look in his eyes was the look of a killer, not a rapist. She was scared but also wanted to live.

So, she stood to her feet, wiped her eyes, and showed him what she chose. He smiled. With time he'd turn her into his new queen.

"The other 3 of em dead?" he asked his killers.

"It wasn't but two bitches upstairs," Kutta answered.

June turned to Black, "where the other one?" Black thought about lying, but the dead body in the doorway kept her honest.

"She upstairs in the same room you found me. She under the bed."

Without being told, Kutta went to retrieve the last lady. An idea came to June's mind as Kutta made it upstairs.

"Don't kill her, bring her to me!" June yelled. Dria tried opening the window as Kutta enter the room, but he smacked her in the back of the head and knocked her out cold. He dragged her down the stairs, as Black looked at her naked body. June smiled and handed her the pistol.

"Her life for yours. It's a loyalty test, to live you gotta have blood on yo hands."

She held the pistol in her hands unable to pull the trigger and take a life. Her hands shook as she thought about what they wanted her to do. She tried handing the gun back, but he shook his head.

"She got 3 seconds to kill her or she get it," June said. Without second thought, Kutta and Bullet pointed their weapons at her. June begin counting, "1....2..."

Before he reached 3, Black aimed at Dria's body, closed her eyes, and pulled the hammer.

Boc! Boc! Boc!

June laughed at how the body shook as it was smacked with bullets. He looked at his new Queen as tears run down her face. She was terrified and helpless. He planned to turn her into Kim 2.0. He grabbed her hand and they left the house. Black followed them out the door, as tears rolled down her face. It took a lot to take a life, but she was a survivor and did what she had to.

(Later That Night)

Bee reread the text Martez sent her an hour ago. *Meet me on Rosenbarry in an hour. Love ya!*

After she received the text, she went and bought a black jumpsuit, then changed in the car. Now she was ready to commit her last murder. After, she wanted to move on with life.

It didn't take long before she arrived on Allied and parked her car. She stepped out with both pretty savages in her waistband. She held them tight, releasing one to pull the hoodie over her head. There was only a short walk to Rosenbarry, and her heart began to race. She spotted his Range Rover, and got low, pulling out her pistols. Her heartbeat was ringing in her ears as she got close enough to fire.

Boc! Boc! Boc! Boc! Boc!

Bee advanced on the car and watched as paint flew off and holes replaced them. She riddled the diver side with bullets.

Boc! Boc! Boc! Boc! Boc! She kept firing as glass ran down on the pavement. She stopped firing and placed one of her firearms in the hoodie pocket before opening the car door with gloved fingers. *What the fuck,* she thought looking inside the empty car.

Reese stepped from around the building. She never saw him coming.

Boom! Boom!

The shots from the Mac 11 clobbered her and sent her slamming into the car face first, knocking one 9mm outta her hand.

Boom! Boom!

He put two more in her spine. Her body slid down the Range Rover and a trail of blood followed. She stared at him as he smiled.

"You a cold-hearted bitch. You would've killed my nigga if he came to meet you."

He laughed, pointing the Mac in her face. He never got the chance to pull the trigger. A van pulled up filled with masked man. They pulled their AK47s and started firing from the passenger window.

Reese took off running as bullets slammed into his back, knocking him to the ground. Two man hopped out with weapons pointed at Bee. She put her hands in the air. She was out manned and out gunned. Thoughts of dying crossed her mind, but at this moment, she welcomed them. She wanted to go see Glory again. Bee looked over and saw one of them exit the van and shoot Reese once in the back of the head. Bee began to pass out as she heard a man yell, "Hurry and get his child before she dies."

To be continued………

Also Available by Bagz of Money Content

Live by It, Die by It (By: Ice Money)

Mercenary (By: Ice Money)

The Ruler of the Red Ruler (By: Kutta)

Block Boyz (By: Juvi)

Team Savage (By Ace Boogie)

Team Savage 2 (By Ace Boogie)

Available at Bagzofmoneycontent.com and most major bookstores.

Made in the USA
Monee, IL
13 October 2022

15820649R00125